## "Aren't you sugar and spice and everything nice!"

Gabe's words were teasing, but his expression became oddly serious.

"You are confusing me with my sisters." Esther grew warm beneath his intense scrutiny.

He tugged gently on her *kapp* ribbon. "I think not. They may be sweet, but I haven't seen a sign of spice among them."

"Sweet is usually enough for most young men."

He didn't take his eyes off her face. "Not me. I like spicy."

She knew she was blushing. "We should go to the house before the storm gets worse."

He took a step back. "You're right."

The rain was coming down in sheets. Esther's *kapp* and her hem were soaked by the time they reached cover.

She laughed as she ran up the steps and shook out her dress. Gabe pulled a handkerchief from his pocket and began to mop her face. "I didn't help much."

She saw his eyes darken. She couldn't look away from him. She didn't want to.

Why hadn't she realized it before now?

She was halfway to falling in love with this wonderful man.

After thirty-five years as a nurse, **Patricia Davids** hung up her stethoscope to become a full-time writer. She enjoys spending her free time visiting her grandchildren, doing some long-overdue yard work and traveling to research her story locations. She resides in Wichita, Kansas. Pat always enjoys hearing from her readers. You can visit her online at patriciadavids.com.

## Books by Patricia Davids

### Love Inspired

#### North Country Amish

*An Amish Wife for Christmas*
*Shelter from the Storm*
*The Amish Teacher's Dilemma*
*A Haven for Christmas*
*Someone to Trust*

### HQN Books

#### The Amish of Cedar Grove

*The Wish*
*The Hope*
*The Prayer*

Visit the Author Profile page
at Harlequin.com for more titles.

# Someone to Trust

## Patricia Davids

**LOVE INSPIRED**
INSPIRATIONAL ROMANCE

# LOVE INSPIRED®
## INSPIRATIONAL ROMANCE

Recycling programs
for this product may
not exist in your area.

ISBN-13: 978-1-335-43079-3

Someone to Trust

Copyright © 2021 by Patricia MacDonald

This edition published by arrangement with Harlequin Books S.A.

For questions and comments about the quality of this book, please contact us at CustomerService@Harlequin.com.

Love Inspired
22 Adelaide St. West, 40th Floor
Toronto, Ontario M5H 4E3, Canada
www.Harlequin.com

**Printed in U.S.A.**

Trust in the Lord with all thine heart;
and lean not unto thine own understanding.
In all thy ways acknowledge him,
and he shall direct thy paths.
—*Proverbs* 3:5–6

This book is lovingly dedicated to nurses,
respiratory therapists, doctors and all medical
personnel working tirelessly to save lives.
May God give you strength and wisdom.
May He guide your hands and hearts
as you bring comfort to all His people.

# *Chapter One*

"I'm happy to tell you that your mother's cousin Waneta is coming for a visit."

Gabe Fisher looked up from the glowing metal wheel rim he was heating in the forge as something in his father's voice caught his attention. Ezekiel Fisher, or Zeke as everyone called him, wasn't overly fond of Waneta, so why was he trying so hard to sound cheerful?

Gabe glanced around the workshop. None of his three brothers seemed to have noticed anything unusual.

Seth continued setting up the lathe to drill out a wheel hub. "That will be nice for *Mamm*. She has been missing her friends back home. I know she and Waneta are close."

Seth was Gabe's younger brother by fifteen minutes. They might look identical, but Seth was the most tenderhearted of the brothers. He was twenty minutes older than no-nonsense Asher, the last Fisher triplet, who was readying wooden spokes to be inserted into the finished wheel hub. Asher bore only a passing resemblance to his two older brothers. Where Gabe and Seth were both blond with blue eyes, Asher was dark-haired with their mother's brown eyes. All three men shared the same tall, muscular frame as their father.

"Is she bringing her new husband to meet the rest of us?" Moses asked, greasing the axle of the buggy they were repairing. At twenty he was the baby brother by four years and the one that looked the most like their mother, with his soft brown curls and engaging grin. He was the only one who hadn't yet joined their Amish church. He was still enjoying his *rumsp-*

*ringa*, the "running around" years most Amish youths were allowed before making their decision to be baptized.

"This isn't the best time for a visit," Asher said, expressing exactly what Gabe had been thinking.

"Apparently your mother and Waneta have been planning this for ages, but she only told me last night. She wanted it to be a surprise for you boys."

Asher's brow furrowed. "Why?"

"You know Waneta. She likes to surprise folks. They should be here later today."

Gabe continued turning the rim in the fire. Both his parents had gone to the wedding, but he and his brothers had been busy keeping the new business running. A business that didn't look like it would support the entire family through another winter. If things didn't improve by the end of the summer, the family would have some hard choices to make.

"They? Her new husband is coming with her, then?" Seth said.

Gabe glanced at his father and saw him draw a deep breath. "He isn't, but his children are."

Seth finally seemed to notice their father's unease and stopped working. "How many children?"

"Five."

"The house will be lively with that many *kinder* underfoot," Moses said. "How old are they?"

"The youngest is ten. The others are closer to your ages," *Daed* said, keeping his eyes averted.

Seth, Asher and Gabe exchanged knowing looks. They shared a close connection that didn't always require words.

Asher's lips thinned as he pinned his gaze on his father. "Would they happen to be *maydels* close to our age?"

Their father didn't answer.

*"Daed?"* the triplets said together. Moses stopped what he was doing and gave them a puzzled look.

Their father cleared his throat. "I believe your mother said they are between twenty and twenty-five. Modest, dutiful daughters, as Waneta described them."

"Courting age," Moses said with a grin.

"Marriageable age." Seth shook his head. "I don't have any interest in courting until we are sure our business will survive."

Gabe crossed his arms over his chest. "Has *Mamm* taken to importing possible brides for us now?"

There was a lack of unmarried Amish women in their new community in northern Maine, but that didn't bother Gabe. Like Seth, his focus was on improving the family's buggy-making and wheel-repair business while expanding the harness-making and leather goods shop he ran next door.

"Tell *Mamm* we can find our own wives," Asher said.

"When we are ready," Seth added.

*Daed* scowled at all the brothers. "That kind of talk is exactly why your mother was worried about sharing this news. She wants you boys to be polite to Waneta's new stepdaughters and nothing more. Show them a nice time while they are here. No one is talking about marriage."

"Marriage is the point of this trip, girls. Do not make me tell your father he wasted his money paying for it. We should be there within the hour."

Esther Burkholder kept her eyes glued to her brother Jonah's hands as the ten-year-old rapidly signed their stepmother's conversation. Seated with Jonah in the back of the van their father had hired to drive them to Maine, Esther couldn't lip-read what Waneta was saying or what her sisters were answering because all she could see was the back of their white Amish *kapps*. Waneta didn't know sign language and showed little interest in learning. Julia, Pamela and Nancy could sign, but they often preferred to talk among themselves, leaving Esther out of the discussion.

Unlike her Deaf friends, who found it isolating to be left out of conversations with hearing family members, Esther normally didn't mind. Even before she lost her hearing, she had preferred to spend time alone. She enjoyed her silent world. All she had to do was close her eyes and nothing intruded on her solitude unless someone touched her. Today was different. She needed to know what Waneta had planned so she could avoid getting caught in the web her stepmother was weaving. Did the poor Fisher brothers know what was about to descend on them?

"I've known these boys since they were babies. The three oldest sons are triplets. They are twenty-four, so a good age to be looking for a wife. Seth is the tenderhearted one who loves children. Pamela, I think you and he could make a match. You have a very caring nature. Asher is the practical one. Julia, I think he might be best suited for you. Your no-nonsense attitude should appeal to him. Nancy, you and Moses, the youngest son, are the same age and not yet baptized. I think the two of you will find you have a lot in common."

"How are we going to tell them apart if they all look alike?"

Jonah rolled his eyes and signed, "Pamela has a good point for once."

"What did Waneta answer?" Esther signed, wishing Jonah would keep his thoughts out of the conversation.

"She said only Gabriel and Seth look alike. Gabriel has a small scar in his right eyebrow. Seth looks like him but no scar. She says Asher and the younger brother are both dark."

He leaned forward over the seat to speak to his stepmother, frustrating Esther. She tugged on his suspender strap. "What are you saying?"

Because she hadn't completely lost her hearing until the age of ten, she spoke almost normally, although she had been told that ability might gradually leave her. She worked hard at practicing her speech so that she wouldn't lose what she had.

Jonah turned back to her. "I asked which

brother Waneta thought would make a good match for you."

Waneta turned in her seat and gave Esther a knowing, sympathetic smile. "I believe the oldest son, Gabriel, would suit you. Sadly, he was jilted when he was twenty and of course was heartbroken. According to my cousin Talitha, he has been put off by the idea of marriage ever since, so I don't hold out much hope for a match. Now I don't want the rest of you to take an interest in only one son. Keep open minds."

Esther knew what Waneta was really saying. None of her cousin's sons would be interested in a deaf woman for a wife. After a moment of self-pity, Esther sat up straight. She wasn't shopping for a husband and certainly not a hearing one. She had a wonderful job working in their community's school for children with disabilities. She and her three close friends who were also Deaf taught twenty hearing-impaired and deaf children in special classes along with assisting the other teachers when needed. She dearly missed her friends and the children already. This trip needed to end quickly.

Jonah touched her shoulder to gain her attention before signing again. "Waneta talks too much. My hands are getting tired. Can I stop?"

Esther smiled and nodded. It had been a long two-day trip from Millersburg, Ohio, and he was growing bored. "Watch out the window. I have read there are many moose and bears in this part of Maine. Perhaps you'll catch a glimpse of one of them," she said.

He eagerly turned his attention outside, leaving Esther alone with her thoughts. This trip was such a waste of time. She sighed and opened the quilted satchel on the floor by her feet. The sketchbook or the sewing projects she'd brought along to occupy her time? She was making new *kapps* for her sisters. Because she enjoyed sewing, she made the clothes for everyone in the family, including her father. She withdrew her sewing kit as fond memories of learning to sew with her mother filled her mind.

She glanced once more at the back of Waneta's head. The woman wasn't a replacement for her mother, but she was good for Esther's father. He smiled more and seemed to enjoy life with her. Because of her father, Esther had tried hard to please Waneta, but she'd failed more often than not. Waneta was impatient with Esther's lack of ability to understand her. So Esther simply stayed out of her way.

Had it been up to her, she wouldn't be on this trip at all. Her father had insisted Esther come along. He told the family he wanted them to see some new country and meet Waneta's favorite cousin and her family. Privately he told Esther he hoped that the trip would bring her and her stepmother closer. He knew there was friction between them. Because she loved her father, Esther had agreed, but two days in a van had certainly not strengthened the bond between her and Waneta.

At least she had gotten to see the ocean

that morning. It had been a stunning sight she would never forget. The highway they had traveled along skirted the beautiful rugged Maine coast from Portsmouth to Brunswick before turning inland. The views of the sparkling waves stretching to the horizon took her breath away. She could never reproduce such beauty with her limited talent for drawing, but she couldn't wait to tell her friends back home about it. She would write as soon as she had the chance.

They had been traveling for almost an hour when Esther felt a change in the vibration of the van and looked up from her sewing. Bessie, their van driver, was pulling off to the side of the road. Jonah began to sign. "I think something is wrong with the engine. Bessie says we should get out and stretch our legs while she takes a look. We are only about a mile from the Fisher farm."

Esther was happy to leave the confines of the van for even a little bit. Outside the afternoon air was fresh with a cool breeze that fluttered the ribbons of her *kapp*. She admired the farmland interspersed with wooded areas that lined either side of a broad valley. She could see a river sparkling in the distance, and closer to the road, a small pond reflected perfectly the clear summer sky and the trees that surrounded it.

Her sister Nancy came to her side. "It's pretty country," she signed.

Esther nodded. "It is. Has Bessie discovered what is wrong?"

"It's nothing she can fix."

Esther glanced up the road. "If it's less than a mile, we can walk."

"Waneta has already sent Jonah ahead to tell the Fishers where we are and what has happened. They will send a buggy or wagon to fetch us and our things."

A car zipped past on the highway, startling Esther. Cars always frightened her if she didn't see them coming first. She looked both ways. There wasn't any other traffic in sight, but she stepped farther back from the roadway. She faced her sister. "Are you as eager to find a husband as Waneta is to find one for you?"

**Nancy shrugged.** "I'm not eager to find a spouse—I just turned twenty—but I'm open to the possibility. Julia and Pamela are more hopeful than I am that the trip will be the answer for them, or maybe they are feeling a tad desperate. Julia will be twenty-six soon, and some folks have started calling her an old maid since she rejected Ogden Martin's proposal in such a public way. Of course she was right to do so. He wasn't a good man.

"Pamela is only a year behind Julia in age. Very few men in our area have shown an interest in us, and Father has discouraged those fellows. He would rather we marry outside our community." **Nancy blushed and stopped signing.**

"Because our incidence of inherited deafness is so high," Esther finished for her. She was aware of her father's feelings, but it still hurt to be reminded that he saw her deafness as an affliction to be avoided rather than embraced. Thankfully his views were not shared by all, but they were shared by the one person who had mattered the most to Esther—Barnabas King, the young man she had fallen in love with and had hoped to marry. Until he'd made his true feelings about her deafness known last Christmas.

She pushed that unhappy memory to the back of her mind. If she ever thought of marrying, she wasn't going to seek a spouse in the hearing world. Only a man who was Deaf could understand the struggles and rewards of existing in a silent world. God would provide such a man for her if that was His plan. If not, she had her job and the children she loved.

Nancy smiled sadly and signed, "All of us want to find someone to love who loves us in return. I won't settle for less, no matter what Father and Waneta have in mind."

"She can be persuasive," Esther said, looking to where her stepmother was talking to Julia and Pamela.

"I know the two of you don't get along, but she isn't a bad sort."

"She's so different from our mother. I know it's wrong to resent her. I'll work on being a better daughter."

"She's calling me. I'm glad to be out of the van, aren't you?" Nancy walked away without waiting for Esther's answer. It wasn't an unusual occurrence.

Esther's gaze was drawn to the pretty picture of the little pond across the way. She couldn't believe her eyes when a moose with enormous antlers stepped out of the forest and waded into the water. She thought he was going to drink, but he plunged his entire head beneath the surface and came up with a mouthful of pond weeds that he munched on contentedly.

Oh, she wished Jonah was here to see this. A real live moose a mere hundred yards away. She had to get a closer look.

Gabe had hitched up the wagon as soon as the boy called Jonah arrived at the farm and explained his family's ride had broken down about a mile away. Now they were both on their way to the van. "Are you excited about spending a few weeks in Maine?" Gabe asked.

"I would rather spend the summer at home playing ball with my friends, but *Daed* said I needed to come along to look after my sisters."

"Do your sisters take a lot of looking after?" Maybe he could learn something useful about his mother's imported bridal prospects.

"Esther needs my help sometimes, but the others don't. They're all going to be too busy trying to find husbands to need me." The kid rolled his eyes.

Gabe grinned. Jonah was exactly the person he needed to pump for information. "All of your sisters are looking for husbands?"

"My stepmother claims she is a *goot* matchmaker and will have them engaged before the end of this trip. She even said we aren't going home until at least two of the girls are promised. I think the whole thing is silly."

"I couldn't agree with you more."

"I'd like to get back to my friends before the ball season is over. I'm the pitcher on our team. Are you looking for a wife?" the boy asked hopefully.

"*Nee*, I'm content being a single fellow."

"So am I. Girls are nothing but trouble. Just ask me. With four sisters, I know what I'm talking about," Jonah said with long-suffering conviction.

Gabe tried hard not to laugh. "How does your stepmother hope to get all your sisters engaged so quickly?"

"I don't know her whole plan. I got tired of listening, but each one is going to concentrate on one brother."

"Who plans to set her sights on me?"

"I don't remember. I was getting pretty tired by then."

A white van with the hood up came into view along with a group of Amish women standing beside it. Gabe pulled the horse and wagon to a stop beside them. Which one was going to concentrate her attention on him? He wished Jonah knew the answer. That way he'd know which sister to avoid. His mother's cousin Waneta came rushing toward him with a cheerful smile.

"Gabriel, it's *goot* to see you again."

He got down from the wagon, determined not to give any of the women undue encouragement. "Nice to see you, too, Waneta. If your stepdaughters will get in the wagon, I'll collect your things."

"Our driver, Bessie, will help. Let me introduce you to my family."

"There will be time for that when everyone is settled at the house," he said and walked to the back of the van where Bessie, a gray-haired *Englisch* woman, was pulling out the luggage. He heard the rumble of a truck approaching and then a horn blaring. He glanced in that direction and saw a woman walking into the roadway. Her gaze was fixed on something in the distance. Didn't she hear the truck? She looked at the ground. The trucker would never be able to stop in time. Gabe dropped the suitcases and dashed toward her.

The truck's brakes squealed. Over the noise Gabe heard screaming behind him. He yelled at her to get off the road. She didn't move a step. He closed his eyes and launched himself toward the woman, knowing they were both going to die.

He hit her and locked his arms around her as they landed on the hard pavement. His momentum sent them rolling to the grassy verge on the opposite side of the road. The wind from the truck tore his hat off. When the vehicle flew past, he kept his eyes closed for several seconds until he realized he was alive.

*Thanks be for Your mercy, Lord.*

He opened his eyes and gazed at the woman beneath him. She stared at him with wide, frightened, amber-colored eyes. She pressed her hands against his chest. "You saved my life."

"Are you hurt?" His arm was starting to sting where he had landed on it.

"I don't know. My head hurts." Her words were slightly slurred.

The rush of adrenaline drained away, leaving Gabe weak and shaken. "Don't move until you're sure. What were you thinking? Didn't you hear the truck? We could've both been killed."

She was staring at his mouth. "I saw a moose. I've never seen one before. I wanted a closer look. Something scared it away. Please let me up."

He rolled off and sat beside her. "It was almost the last thing you saw."

Her family surrounded them and helped her to her feet. They were chattering and motioning with their hands as they hugged her and checked her for injures. It dawned on Gabe that they were using sign language. At least that's what he thought it was. Was the woman deaf? Was that why she hadn't heard the trucker's horn or his shouts?

The big rig's driver had managed to stop the truck a hundred yards down the road. He came running up to Gabe. "Are you okay? Is she all right? I couldn't stop in time. She just walked out in front of me. Man, what you did was the bravest thing I've ever seen."

"Or the most foolish."

"I've always heard there's very little difference between the two." The man patted his chest. "That took ten years off my life. If you had been a second slower—"

Visibly upset, the man sat down in the grass beside Gabe. "Are you folks Amish? I've heard some of you have moved here."

"We are."

"After today, I might trade my truck in for a horse and buggy."

"You won't haul near as much lumber that way."

The man chuckled. "You're right. Maybe I'll just slow down and keep an eye out for folks like you."

"We would appreciate that."

Jonah, pale and shaken, left his sister and came to sit beside Gabe. "You saved Esther's life. *Danki*, but it should have been me. I'm the one *Daed* sent to look after her. I reckon I didn't do such a *goot* job."

Gabe draped his arm over the boy's shoulders. "You brought me here. Looks like that was *Gott's* plan for both of us."

"I just remembered something."

"What?" Gabe asked.

The child looked up with his eyes full of wonder. "Esther is the one *Mamm* picked for you."

# Chapter Two

Esther couldn't stop shaking. She was afraid her knees wouldn't hold her up much longer. Her shoulders, her hip and the back of her head were starting to hurt. Tomorrow she would likely be black and blue all over, but she was alive. God be praised. She leaned heavily on Nancy's arm.

Julia immediately took charge and signed as she spoke so everyone would know what she wanted. "Let's get Esther to the wagon."

Julia turned to Gabriel. "Are you able to drive the team? If not I will."

"I can drive." Gabriel got up with a grimace as Jonah helped him to his feet. The truck driver added a steadying hand to his back. Gabriel nodded his thanks.

"You're hurt," Esther said, pointing to his arm. His shirt was torn from his elbow to his shoulder. There was blood dripping from his fingers. She swallowed hard against the pain of knowing her disability had almost cost him his life as well as her own. How could she have been so foolish?

He tried to look at the injury, but the blood was soaking his shirtsleeve. "It's nothing."

Esther was able to read his lips, but Jonah signed for her, as well.

"It's more than nothing. Let me see." Julia made a quick examination. "That's a nasty gash. You might need stitches." She turned to Bessie but didn't sign, so Esther had no idea what she was saying. Bessie hurried to the van and came back a few moments later with a first-aid kit.

Esther was grateful for her older sister's competence. Once Julia had a dressing on

Gabriel's wound, she ushered everyone into the wagon, where Bessie had loaded their luggage. Esther sat facing Gabe as he leaned against the side boards of the wagon bed. He cradled his injured arm across his chest. Jonah got in beside him and handed him his hat.

"*Danki.*"

Esther carefully studied his face.

He was a good-looking man with blond hair and sky blue eyes. He had strong features, a square chin and a nicely shaped mouth. She thought he must smile often, for he had tiny laugh lines bracketing his lips. "I'm sorry you got hurt saving me. I was careless."

"I hope you're more careful in the future. I might not be handy." He glanced at her brother. "I don't know sign language. Can you tell her that for me?"

"Esther can speech-read pretty well."

"I thought she read lips."

"Some call it speech-reading, but calling it lip-reading is fine. I guess that's the most common term. It's more about interpreting expressions and face muscles' movements. You have to look directly at her when you talk. She can get the gist of what you're saying, if not every word. I'll sign for you."

*"Danki."*

He looked ill at ease. Esther was used to having hearing people feel uncomfortable around her, but she didn't want this man to feel that way. She owed him too much. How could she repay such bravery?

"You are Gabriel, am I right?" She smiled to put him at ease.

"Folks call me Gabe."

"We haven't actually met. I am Esther." She gestured to the front of the wagon, where her stepmother sat beside her sister on the bench seat. "You already know Waneta. Julia is driving. She is my oldest sister. This is Pamela and Nancy." She indicated the women sitting on their suitcases behind the wagon seat.

"I'm happy to make everyone's acquaintance." He nodded to her sisters, but his eyes held wariness, not happiness, as his gaze slid over them. Something wasn't right.

She looked at Jonah and signed, "What did you tell him about us?"

"I don't know what you mean," he signed back without speaking.

Having a conversation in sign without explaining what was being said to Gabe might be considered rude, but Esther didn't care. "Jonah, the truth."

"I might have mentioned Waneta's plan to find everyone husbands."

Esther pressed her lips together tightly. "Why would you do that?"

"It just slipped out," he signed with an apologetic grimace.

"Tell me you didn't mention that I was looking for a husband."

Jonah looked away and then back at her. "I did say Waneta had picked him out for you."

"Jonah, how could you?" Esther closed her eyes and leaned her head back to pretend she was alone in the world. No sights, no sounds, no humiliating suspicious looks from the man who had just saved her life. Somehow she would have to make it clear to him—when her stepmother and her sisters weren't listening in—that she wasn't husband hunting.

Someone tapped her foot. She opened her eyes to see Gabe frowning at her. "Are you okay?"

"I'm fine." She forced herself to smile. Humiliated, bruised from head to toe and stuck in Maine. She was about as far from fine as she could get. A headache began pounding away fiercely at what few wits she had left.

Gabe wanted to know what she and her brother had been saying to each other. Whatever it was, it made her blush. Her cheeks were as red as the barn he had helped paint in the spring. He suspected the conversation had something to do with him. Otherwise, why wouldn't she share it? Jonah looked guilty and contrite. None of the sisters spoke.

Waneta, on the other hand, hadn't

stopped talking about his prompt action, his quick thinking and his disregard for his own safety since she had climbed to the wagon seat. Her voice had become almost a whine, like the sound of the band saw running in the buggy shop.

Julia drove the wagon into the farmyard. His family came out of the house to greet them.

His father took hold of the horse's bridle as he looked at Gabe and frowned. "What has happened?"

"It was the most frightening thing, Cousin." Waneta got down and threw her arms around Gabe's mother then launched into her dramatic version of the story as Gabe's brothers helped him and the women out of the wagon. Gabe's mother's face grew pale as she listened.

"I'm okay, *Mamm*." Gabe touched her shoulder. "It's just a scrape."

"He needs stitches," Julia said, getting down. "Is there a physician nearby?"

"There is a new clinic in Fort Craig. I'll

hitch up the buggy." Asher jogged toward the corral to get their buggy horse, Topper.

"I don't need a doctor," Gabe declared. He'd lost enough working time already.

Moses helped Esther down from the wagon. The color left her face, and she crumpled. She would have hit the ground if Moses hadn't swept her up in his arms. "I think this one might."

Moses carefully lowered Esther to the ground. His mother and her sisters gathered around. Gabe was relieved when her eyes fluttered open. She frowned. "What happened?"

"You fainted," her sister Nancy told her.

She raised her hand to her brow. "My head hurts."

"We're going to take you and Gabe to a doctor," Julia said and signed.

"I'm sorry I'm being so much trouble." She closed her eyes again. Gabe knew how hard he had struck her when he tackled her. He had tried to protect her when they hit the ground, but she could easily have serious injuries.

Seth quickly unhitched their workhorse from the wagon and took him to the barn. Asher had Topper hitched to the buggy in a matter of minutes and drove him up to the house. Gabe's mother got in and had Moses lift Esther in beside her. Gabe climbed in and sat across from the two women. His mother looked out the door. "There is room for you, Cousin Waneta."

Waneta took a step backward. "Nancy should go with her. I haven't learned enough sign language to be of any help."

Gabe's father climbed in and took the driving lines. He looked at his sons. "Help our guests get settled. We will be back as quick as we can. Topper, step trot." The horse took off down the lane.

Gabe hadn't had a chance to tell his brothers what he knew about Waneta's matchmaking plans. He would as soon as he returned. If his brothers wanted to find wives, that was up to them to decide, but they should be warned they were now the targets of their mother's matchmaking cousin and her brood.

The trip to the clinic in Fort Craig took almost an hour. Esther was seen immediately. Gabriel ended up waiting thirty minutes before the physician was able to get to him. When the young man in a white lab coat entered the room, Gabe's father, who had been waiting with him, sat up straight. "How is the woman who came in with us?"

"She gave her permission for me to share her condition with your family because she knew you were worried so I can tell you she has a concussion. I told your wife and her sister that someone should be with her around the clock for the next twenty-four hours and to wake her at regular intervals to make sure her symptoms aren't getting worse. She could lapse into a coma if there is bleeding in her brain. In that case she will need immediate surgery. After that I want her to rest for at least another day."

The doctor read through the notes the nurse who had admitted Gabe had written. He looked at Gabe. "I want you to lie down on the table."

"I hit her pretty hard," Gabe admitted as he complied.

"She told me. She's thankful it was you and not the truck." He put his stethoscope in his ears and listened to Gabe's heart and lungs and pressed several places on his belly. "Does that hurt? Do you have pain anywhere else?"

Gabe shook his head. "I have a few aches and bruises. Nothing more than that."

The doctor seemed satisfied. "Okay. Let's take a look at this arm." He unwound the bandages. "Ouch. Oh, this is going to need stitches. I'll get the nurse in here to help me."

When he left, Gabe's father paced to the door and back. "He sounds concerned about Esther."

"So am I," Gabe admitted.

"Waneta should have come with her."

"You heard her say she doesn't sign well enough."

"She'd known the family for more than a year before she married Carl. You'd think she would have made a point of learning to talk to the child even before the wedding."

"Maybe it is a hard thing to learn, and Esther is hardly a child."

*Daed* shook his head. "Even if it is difficult, that's not a good excuse. Your mother has had concerns about their relationship. Just things she has gathered from Waneta's letters. She claims the girl is stubborn and resents her trying to take her mother's place."

"She's a grown woman. Does that seem likely?"

"Who can say? I think there is more to the story."

The doctor and the nurse returned, ending their conversation, but it gave Gabe something to think about. If Esther was unhappy with her new stepmother, maybe she was eager to find a husband and get out of the house. He could sympathize with her, but he wasn't going to give her a hand with that. He'd already done enough by saving her life.

It didn't take long to get ten stitches in his arm. Hearing that he wasn't to use his arm for several days was disappointing.

"We can spare you from the repair shop," his father said as he helped Gabe slip into his shirt after the doctor and nurse left the room. "Work in your harness shop can wait a few days, too."

"The Potato Blossom Festival is only three weeks away. I've already paid for a booth at the event to sell my leather goods. As of now I don't have enough pieces ready to make it worth my while."

"Your plans to expand your harness business with other leather goods is ambitious, but don't think the fate of the family rests in your hands. We will get by. *Gott* provides. We have enough repairs lined up to take care of our needs."

"*Daed*, you know as well as I do that we won't be able to make the loan payment on our land in August unless we can bring in additional income. Seth and Asher are talking about moving to the city and taking jobs there."

His father sighed heavily. "That would break your mother's heart. I brought us here to get away from the influences of so many *Englisch* moving into our part of Pennsylvania. To have my sons find work in a factory is not what I wanted. I thought more Amish from our area would follow us here. I thought we would be the only buggy builders in this part of Maine and that we would have more work than we could handle. It pains me to say I was wrong. Two of the new families left last winter because the weather was so harsh. The New Covenant Amish community is too small to support us. If we had stayed in Pennsylvania, at least the boys could have found work in the factories with other Amish men and women. Here they will be alone among outsiders."

Gabe laid his hand on his father's shoulder. "If I can sell enough of my leather goods to the *Englisch* tourists, and if we have a decent potato harvest, we will make the loan payment and have another year together. More Amish will come. This is a fine place you brought us to, *Daed*."

The thousands of tourists who attended the Potato Blossom Festival each year were Gabe's best chance of earning the money the family needed. He was sure his quality wallets, belts, ax and knife sheaths, among other things, would appeal to the festivalgoers. If he could finish more items in time.

Out in the waiting room, he saw his mother sitting with Esther and Nancy. The sisters were conversing in sign language with a nurse. Gabe had seen people using sign language before, but he hadn't known any of them personally until now. It looked complicated.

Esther caught sight of him and smiled. "How are you?"

He patted his arm gingerly. "Almost as good as new. What about you?" He gestured to her head. Her hair was down and loosely braided, but she had her kapp on.

"I still have a headache, but I don't feel

faint anymore." She touched her prayer covering. "I had to take my hair down for the X-ray. The doctor thought the padding my hair provided may have saved me from a worse injury. This is Nurse Heather. She knows sign language."

"I see that."

Heather touched Esther's arm to gain her attention then handed her several pieces of paper. "These are instructions for you and your family," she said as she signed. "Things to watch for. Do you have any questions for me?"

Nancy and Esther looked at each other and shook their heads. "We will take good care of her," Nancy said. "I'm so glad you know ASL. It makes things much easier for my sister."

"What is ASL?" his mother asked.

Heather smiled at her. "American Sign Language. My husband and I had to learn it when we realized our son had been born deaf. Because of that we foster two twin girls who are also deaf, and we hope to adopt them. What we once saw as a tragedy was instead a blessing in disguise for us and for our girls."

"Were they also born deaf?" Gabe's mother asked.

"Their hearing loss is due to untreated ear infections when they were five. Their mother was a single woman with a drug problem. Sadly the girls suffered from neglect and abuse at her hands. However, they are happy and healthy now. It was amazing how quickly they learned to sign. We are investigating bone-anchored hearing devices for them."

"What is that?" his mother asked.

"A small metal post is surgically implanted in the bone behind the ear. When the bone is healed, a hearing device simply snaps onto it. Sounds, which are only vibrations, are transmitted to the inner ear through the bone. It won't help people with nerve deafness like my son, but my grandfather has age-acquired hearing loss in both ears, and eventually his hearing aids no longer helped. He retreated from his friends and became depressed. He had the surgery, and it has made a world of difference for him. He enjoys being around people again. The girls will wear temporary devices held against the bony place behind their ears with soft headbands for several months before having any surgery. We want to see if it is the right choice for them. I have some literature on the procedure if you would like."

"Thank you, but it isn't something I am interested in," Esther said.

"Are you sure?" Nancy asked.

"Very sure." Esther looked away.

Gabe and his mother exchanged puzzled glances. Why wouldn't Esther want to learn about something that could let her hear? He wished he knew more about deafness. Maybe she knew she couldn't be helped.

The nurse turned to Gabe. "You need to come back in a week to have those sutures removed. I've made an appointment for you." She handed him a small card.

*"Danki."* He took it from her.

"Okay, you are free to go."

He opened the door. His mother rose to her feet and took Esther by the arm to shepherd her outside. Nancy hung back and turned to the nurse. "I'd like some information on the device you spoke about."

"Of course." Heather went behind her counter and handed Nancy a brochure. "There is a phone number you can call."

"Thank you." Nancy slipped the paper in her purse and hurried outside.

On the return trip, Esther sat with her eyes closed and her head leaned against Nancy's shoulder. Neither sister said a word.

When the buggy stopped, Esther sat up. Her furrowed brow told Gabe she was in pain. He got out and gripped her arm to steady her as she got down. She leaned heavily on him.

His mother had noticed her discomfort, too. "Nancy, why don't you take Esther upstairs and let her lie down? She looks worn out. Your room is at the end of the hall."

"All right." Nancy signed something to

Esther, who merely nodded, and they both went in the house.

While his father put the buggy and horse away, Gabe followed his mother inside. He found Asher and Seth in the living room playing a board game with the two oldest Burkholder sisters and Jonah. The women were smiling and laughing. Waneta sat in the corner with a smug look on her face. She rose to her feet when Gabe's mother entered the room.

"How is your dear brave son, Cousin Talitha?"

Was it odd that she didn't ask about her stepdaughter first?

"He will be fine. Esther needs to be watched closely for the next two days. I had Nancy take her up to their room."

Waneta pulled a long face. "That girl is always making more work for her family. Her carelessness is the reason your son was hurt, and I'm so very sorry."

Gabe scowled at Waneta's unkind comment about Esther but held his tongue.

"All is forgiven," his mother said. "We

will speak no more about it. By God's grace, both our children were spared."

Gabe looked at his brothers. "Have you finished the wheel for Jedidiah Zook? *Daed* told him it would be ready today."

"We were just about to go out and finish it," Seth said. The men murmured their apologies to the women and got up.

"What did the doctor say about you?" Asher asked as they stepped outside.

"He put in ten stitches and said not to use the arm for several days. I get the stitches out in a week."

As soon as they were out of earshot of the house, Gabe stopped walking. His brothers turned to face him. "I want you to know that matchmaking is the only reason Waneta has brought her stepdaughters along on this visit. Be aware that they are all husband hunting."

A frown appeared on Asher's face. "They seem like nice women, but I'm not on the lookout for a wife."

Seth shrugged. "I wouldn't mind getting to know them better. Just because Wa-

neta and *Mamm* have hatched a matchmaking plot between them doesn't mean
it's a bad idea. Waneta has known us since
we were babies. If she thinks her stepdaughters would suit us, we should keep
an open mind."

Gabe scowled at him. "You have
changed your tune since this morning.
I've got better things to do than to start
courting someone who lives in another
state. If our business doesn't improve, we
could all be taking jobs in the city."

"We put our faith in *Gott*. He will provide," Seth said quietly.

Gabe felt his brother's gentle rebuke.
"The Lord sends the rain and the sun to
make our garden grow, but we must still
hoe the weeds." It would take faith and
effort to keep the family together. The
brothers had never been apart for more
than a few days. Gabe would do everything in his power to see that didn't happen.

Asher crossed his arms over his chest.

"We won't neglect our work because we have visitors, Gabe."

"I know. I'm sorry if I sound cranky. Pay me no mind. What did our cousin and her stepdaughters have to say?"

"*Goot* things about you." Moses grinned.

Asher chuckled. "I thought Waneta was never going to stop praising your brave deed. You must be more careful, *brudder*. That could have been the end of the Fisher triplets, and twins are just so common."

"I did what any of you would have done, and you know it. Come on, I'll give you a hand with the wheel. I've got one good one left."

They chuckled at his little joke and went into the workshop at the side of the barn. Gabe glanced over his shoulder at the second-story room where he knew Esther had gone. He caught sight of her standing by the window.

He wanted her to be okay. He wanted to see her smile. It appeared that things weren't good between Esther and her new stepmother. Family was second only to

God in Amish life. Gabe never had to worry that his wouldn't stand by him.

Esther raised her hand in a brief wave before turning away. It was a shame she was trapped in a silent world. Why hadn't she taken the information about a device that could let her hear? And why had her sister taken it after Esther left the clinic?

## Chapter Three

Esther woke early the next morning. There wasn't a place on her body that didn't hurt, but at least her headache was manageable. The moment she moved, she remembered everything that had happened yesterday. The vibration under her feet that had confused her, then the glimpse she'd had of the truck from the corner of her eye when she knew it was too late to run. The impact against her that wasn't hard steel but rather muscle and bone. When she had opened her eyes and found herself looking up at Gabe's face, she could hardly believe she wasn't dead.

She had been given a second chance at life by an amazingly brave man.

How was Gabe this morning? Was he as sore as she was? She thought again of his sky blue eyes and his pretty mouth. Maybe it wasn't right to call a man's mouth pretty, but she spent a lot of time looking at that part of people's faces, and she knew a pretty one when she saw it.

She sat up and stretched her stiff muscles. Her brush with death had given her a new appreciation for life. She might be sore, but she wasn't going to waste this precious new day lying in bed. If she didn't get up, all she would think about was Gabe—his strength, his kindness and his smile. It was all that had occupied her mind yesterday whenever she woke. It was probably only natural given the way they had met, but he was occupying far too much of her thoughts. The thing to do was to get moving and work out the kinks from her body and her mind.

She glanced around the room and saw her sisters were all still in their cots. Two of them had their pillows over their heads, so she guessed that Waneta had been snoring. It was a complaint they had shared about her on this trip and one thing Esther was glad hadn't disturbed her rest.

She dressed quickly and went to the window. There was a faint pale pink light across the eastern sky. The sun would be up in an hour. What to do until then? Going back to sleep was out of the question, but a solitary walk in the predawn light held an allure. She would take her sketchbook in case she happened upon some unfamiliar flowers. She slipped the pad and her colored pencils into a quilted pouch and slung it over her shoulder, wincing at the movement but undeterred.

Downstairs she saw Talitha starting coffee in the kitchen. The family would be up soon if they weren't already outside doing chores. She didn't want to bother her hostess, so she slipped out the front door.

The morning air was cool and crisp. It might be summer in Maine, but the air felt like early fall at home in central Ohio. She drew a deep breath. The smells of pine and wood smoke came to her on a gentle breeze. A walk on this beautiful morning that the Lord had made after resting in bed was exactly what she needed. But to where?

She looked down the lane toward the highway. Would the moose return to his feeding spot? She'd had so little time to admire the massive creature yesterday. She would take a chance and see if her curiosity was rewarded.

Walking down to the highway, she followed along the verge of the road until she came to the place where the van had broken down. There was a puddle of oil in the grass, but the van was gone. Bessie must have had it towed away.

Esther hoped the repair wasn't costly. Bessie made extra money driving the Amish in their community. She had agreed to this trip because she was meeting some friends in Bar Harbor for a two-week vacation. She had promised to check with Waneta before she returned to Ohio in case the family was ready to go back with her. Waneta thought they would be staying a month or more and had said she would make other arrangements. Esther prayed two weeks was all she would have to spend away from her Deaf friends and the job she loved. Maybe by then she could convince Waneta to let her return with Bessie.

After looking carefully in both directions, she stepped out onto the highway. The moment her feet touched the pavement, she shuddered. How long would it be before she could walk down the road again without worrying about being struck by a vehicle? Or tackled by a large man?

Poor Gabe. She would have to find a way to repay his daring action. And she would have to find the right time to tell him she was not husband hunting.

She checked both directions three times as she hurried across the road to the edge of the pond. She sat down, drew her knees up and wrapped her arms around them as she waited for the sun to come up.

\* \* \*

Gabriel raised his arm to hang up his hat and stopped halfway at the pull of his stitches and sore muscles. He had gone out to help with the morning chores, but his brothers and his father had made him go back into the house. Switching his hat to his other hand, he hung it up and turned around. The kitchen was full of women chatting and laughing. His mother looked happy amid the company. He searched the room but didn't see Esther. He didn't blame her for sleeping in. It had been a wildly dramatic day yesterday.

He went into the living room until breakfast was ready. He found Jonah reading one of his favorite books.

"That's a good adventure story." He gestured toward the novel.

"It is," Jonah said and signed something.

"Do you always do that?"

Jonah looked up. "Do what?"

"Sign although your sister isn't in the room?"

"Did I? Habit, I reckon. I want to make

sure that Esther knows what's going on, especially when she isn't with her Deaf friends. And that's Deaf with a capital *D*. They are an amazing group of people. To them deafness isn't a disability. Sometimes my sisters forget that Esther is around and they don't sign. She so quiet, so it's easy to do."

"She speaks very well. Was she able to hear at one time?"

Jonah closed his book, keeping one finger in between the pages. "*Daed* told me she became completely deaf when she was ten, but she started to lose her hearing when she was eight. We have two deaf cousins, but my folks didn't think much about it until Esther became hard of hearing. The doctors told them it was an inherited type of deafness that doesn't show up until the child is older, but she was born with it. They learned more of their children might become deaf."

"Does that mean you could lose your hearing?"

"It's possible. Since I'm already ten,

*Daed* thinks it has skipped me as it did the rest of the girls."

"Maybe it's not my business, but I noticed that Esther and Waneta don't seem as close as your other sisters."

"Esther likes to be alone. I mean, she helps at the school near us for special-needs children. She loves doing that, but when she's in a group of hearing people, she just retreats into a corner or against the wall. It's hard to look at everyone's face at once to try to guess what they're saying."

"What do you mean, guess? I thought she could lip-read?"

"With people she knows well, she can get most of what they are saying, but strangers are harder. Only about half the words we use can be understood by someone who lip-reads. The person has to be looking right at Esther and speaking slowly. Waneta has a habit of putting her fingers on her lips and tapping them and speaking very quickly. Waneta thinks Esther misunderstands her on purpose."

Gabriel heard his father and brothers come in. Nancy stepped into the room. "Jonah, tell Esther breakfast is ready."

"Okay. Is she upstairs?"

"*Nee*, she was already gone when I got up. I thought she must be with you."

He shook his head. "I haven't seen her this morning."

"She has to be around somewhere. Look in the garden. You know how she likes flowers." Nancy turned on her heels and went back to the kitchen.

Gabe had read through the information the nurse had given Esther's family. One of the complications they were to look for was confusion. Had she become confused and wandered off before anyone was up? People in their right senses could easily become lost in these woods if they were unfamiliar with the area. He got to his feet. "I'll help you look for her."

Outside he opened his mouth to call her name and closed it again. That wouldn't help. She couldn't hear him.

"You take the garden. I'll check in the barn. She likes animals," Jonah said.

Gabe didn't find her in his mother's flower garden. There was no sign that she'd been there. The dew was heavy and undisturbed on the grass walkway. She would have left footprints if she had walked along it. He returned to the front of the house and scanned the farmyard. Where would she go? She couldn't hear him calling. She hadn't heard the blare of the semi's horn yesterday. Surely she wouldn't go back to the highway. Then he remembered something she had said. She had wanted to see the moose.

Jonah said she loved animals. Enough to try to see a moose again? It seemed unlikely, but he didn't have anywhere else to start. He called for Jonah and heard the boy answer, "I haven't found her."

"I'm going down to the highway. You keep looking around here."

"Okay."

Gabriel walked quickly down the lane and followed the edge of the highway until he came within sight of the pond. She was there. Sitting in the grass with a sketch pad on her lap while a huge moose grazed on water plants a hundred yards from her. He let out a breath of relief.

He crossed the highway, sat down beside her and touched her shoulder. She turned to him with a huge grin on her face. "Do you see him? Isn't he beautiful?"

Impressive, yes, but not as beautiful as her face in the morning sun. Her amazing amber eyes sparkled with delight, like honey in a clear glass jar, only warmer. Momentarily at a loss for words, he looked down and cleared his throat. "Breakfast is ready."

He felt her hand under his chin as she lifted his face and turned it toward her. "I can't see what you are saying unless you are looking at me."

"I said breakfast is ready if you're hungry."

She turned back to the moose. "*Nee*, I could sit here all day watching this fellow. He's so big. He can keep his head underwater for the longest time. I wanted to get closer, but I wasn't sure it was safe." She looked at him again. "I wouldn't want to force you to save my life again."

Gabe smiled, rose and pulled her to her feet. He wanted to make sure she could see his lips. "A cow with a calf can be dangerous. As can the males during the mating season, but this time of year they are mostly interested in food. You are safe enough at this distance."

"Say that again, and slower, please."

"You're safe as long as he's eating. Speaking of food, I'm hungry. Now that I have found you, I'm not going back without you. Your family was worried."

She shook her head. "*Nee*, they were not. They're used to my odd behaviors. They know I'll turn up eventually."

"Okay, then, I was worried."

"Why?"

"You hit your head hard enough to get a concussion. The papers the doctor sent said confusion was one of the signs we should look for." Her gaze drifted back to the moose.

Gabriel cupped her cheek and turned her face toward him, remembering he had to speak slowly and distinctly. "I was worried you might have become confused and gotten lost."

He realized how close he was to her. His hand still cupped her delicate cheek. If he bent closer, he could kiss her softly smiling lips.

Why would he even think such a thing? He released her abruptly. "We need to go back before my rumbling stomach scares the poor moose into thinking I want his waterlilies."

"I am a little hungry, now that you mention it."

He rubbed his hands on his pant legs to erase the feel of her soft, warm skin against his palm. She caught his arm before he turned away. "I have something to tell you."

"Okay, I'm listening."

"My stepmother believes she is a wondrous *goot* matchmaker. I know Jonah mentioned that she had picked you as a potential spouse for me. I'm grateful for what you did. You've been very kind and I'm sure you would make a fine husband. For someone. Just not for me. I can't—I won't begin a romantic relationship with a hearing man. It's too hard. For me and for him. I hope you understand. I owe you a great deal, my life in fact, but all I can repay you with is honesty."

Gabe was taken aback by her candor. "I appreciate that."

"I'm so glad to clear this up. My sisters hope to wed one day soon, so if you'd like to take one of them out while we are here, that would be more than acceptable."

He managed a wry smile. "I am not looking for a wife."

She tipped her head to the side. "Why not?"

He thought about explaining his business plans but remembered her brother saying she might only understand half of what he was trying to tell her. He would need Jonah or one of her sisters to help. "I'll show you after breakfast," he said slowly, hoping she understood.

Esther walked beside Gabriel with a much lighter heart. Even her headache was nearly gone. Now that he knew she wasn't angling to become his wife, perhaps they could enjoy a friendship while she was staying with his family. She liked him and wanted to get to know him better. She cast a covert glance his way. Was it only because he had saved her, or was there something else that attracted her to him? She wasn't sure.

And if she did find him attractive, there was nothing wrong with that. She could admire a fine horse without having to own it or a cute puppy without taking it home. She could enjoy the company of a handsome man without thinking of him in a romantic fashion. She realized how liberating it was to have finally admitted the truth to someone. She didn't want a hearing husband.

At breakfast she met the rest of the family. Zeke Fisher was a burly man in his early fifties with streaks of silver in his blond hair and beard. Seth bore a striking resemblance to Gabe, but she could have told them apart without the tiny scar in Gabe's eyebrow. Seth's face was softer, less angular than Gabe's, but he had the same sky blue eyes. If he was uncomfortable with her deafness, it didn't show. He made an effort to converse with her through her sisters. Asher and Moses, on the other hand, reacted the way most people did when they met her. They kept their eyes averted except for covert glances and they avoided speaking to her. They weren't trying to be unkind. They were simply uncomfortable. She understood but wished she could slip away to the moose pond again. He hadn't minded her presence at his breakfast. Animals were much more accepting than people.

She was buttering her toast when Nancy touched her arm to get her attention. Everyone was looking at her. She laid the knife aside. "What?"

Nancy spoke and signed, "Several friends of the Fishers are hosting a picnic for us in a few days at the school. Waneta doesn't want you to feel you need to go."

Holding back a grin with difficulty, Esther rubbed her brow. She was being given a chance to say no. She should take it. "I will have to wait and see."

"I'll stay with you if you don't feel up to going." Nancy said.

"*Nee*, I don't want to spoil anyone else's fun. I'll be fine here alone."

Nancy shook her head. "You won't be alone. Gabe isn't going."

Esther looked at him. "Why not?"

"I have my leatherwork to catch up on," he said, staring straight at her.

She tipped her head slightly and watched his mouth. "What kind of work?"

"Leather goods. I will show you my shop when you are feeling up to it."

She didn't need Nancy to sign—she

understood him. It was unusual to find someone she could speech-read so readily.

"I would like that. I feel well enough at the moment. My headache is bearable." She smiled at him and finished buttering her toast.

After breakfast Gabe led her and Jonah to his workshop beside the barn. He opened the door with a flourish. "This is where I make harnesses and other leather goods."

The smell of leather and oils delighted her. She gazed about in awe. There were harnesses and straps of every kind for working horses, but it was the small items that caught her attention. Wallets, key chains, dog collars of every size with matching leashes. There were sheaths for knives and hatchets as well as tool belts. There were even small boots. She picked one up, thinking it was the wrong shape for a child's moccasin. She held one out to him. "What are these?"

She looked to Jonah as he signed Gabe's answer. "Dog boots. In the winter there are a lot of dogsled races here and in neighboring areas of Canada. The dogs wear boots to protect their feet from the ice and snow while they are running."

"I never knew that."

She touched some of the belts and ran her fingers along the perfectly aligned stitches. "You have a steady hand."

She caught sight of a familiar apparatus and stepped over to it. She turned to grin at him. "This appears to be the moose-size version of my humble sewing machine."

He patted the top of it. "It's old and has seen better days, but it is hand operated and can stitch through three thicknesses of leather."

"And this?" She pointed to a set of rollers that resembled the wringer on her washing machine only with different size grooves in it.

"It's a creasing machine. Let me show you how it works. I'll make a strap." He picked up a tool. "This is a draw knife. I use it to cut strips of leather from the tanned hide. Once I have a strip the length

I want, I feed it into the creaser. It comes out perfectly trimmed with creases that give me a stitch line as a pattern pressed into the leather. Then I take it to the sewing machine."

He demonstrated how to position the piece, set the pressure foot and then reached to pull down a lever with a ball on the end. He stopped with a grimace, unable to raise his injured right arm high enough. He motioned for Jonah to operate the lever and set the first stitch. With Jonah's help he stitched about four inches and stopped. "That's how it's done."

"May I try it?" Esther asked, intrigued by the machine.

"Sure." He showed her how to set the stitch length and how to make a turn, then he stepped back. She quickly found the rhythm and was able to complete the strap.

He snipped the threads and examined her work. "*Goot*. Very straight. Nice and even."

She grinned at his praise. "I told you I

like to sew. This is very interesting. How do you sell these things? I didn't see any signs advertising them. Do you have a shop in town or someone who sells them for you?" She looked to Jonah to sign Gabe's answer.

"These are the inventory I'm taking to the Potato Blossom Festival in three weeks. I paid for a booth there, and I plan to sell them during the festival."

She raised one eyebrow. "You can't run a business on a single festival."

He tipped his head toward her and grinned, deepening the laugh lines bracketing his mouth. "You are absolutely right. I will need a storefront in time. There isn't enough room in this building right now, but it will be easy enough to add onto it."

She enjoyed his enthusiasm. She could see he liked his work. He had an artist's gift, something she hadn't expected. "Have you thought about selling on the internet? I ask because I have a friend who makes reed baskets. She sells them online. She hired a manager, an *Englisch* woman, to handle the orders and the computer side of her business."

He sobered. "It's an idea I mean to explore in the future. For now, I plan to hand sell my items."

"If your church district allows it, you should look into it sooner rather than later."

He shrugged and turned away. She tapped on Jonah's shoulder to relay Gabe's words to her. Jonah scowled. "I know. He said a man needs to make a living to feed his family and help in the community, but he doesn't need to make a lot of money. If he has a business that makes a profit, he doesn't need to go bigger."

He was right. There was a lot to like about Gabe Fisher. He believed in living the values taught by their church. God first, family second, community third. He would make a fine husband for a woman who could hear. She checked the pang of self-pity that hit her and turned her attention to the enormous sewing machine. When she had her emotions under control, she smiled at him and gestured around the room. "How much more inventory do you want to take with you to the festival?"

"About twice as much. My problem has been finding the time. Spring and summer are busy times for buggy and wheel repair with all the farmwork underway. I can't slack on the work that is paying our bills while I daydream about earning more." He flexed his injured arm gingerly. "This is not going to let me catch up."

Suddenly she saw a way to repay some of his kindness. It was so simple and something she liked to do, anyway. "Maybe I could help."

Both his eyebrows shot up. "You? How?"

"I'm known as a good seamstress. I could do your stitching while you did the tooling on the pieces. Some of the items in here don't need tooling. The dog leashes are just simple stitching. So are the belts. Even some of the gun holsters and knife sheaths don't require much tooling."

She held up a small holster. "Take this piece. I could add a concho threaded with leather fringe for decoration and sew the two pieces together in no time. I wouldn't mind helping."

She saw his indecision and put the holster down. "You gave me my life back yesterday. I feel this might repay you in some small way. Please allow me to help."

He rubbed his hand across his chin as he considered her offer. He didn't look convinced. She held her breath, wanting him to say yes. Only because she wanted to stay busy until she could return home. Not because the thought of spending time in Gabe's company was appealing. Even if it was.

# Chapter Four

Gabe considered Esther's offer to help. He looked around his workroom. It was filled with his cutting table, stacks of tanned hides, rollers, presses, machines to stitch and mold leather. There was barely room for him to move around as it was without adding another person underfoot. Two, since she would need Jonah to convey what he said.

Anyway, how much help could she be if she wasn't familiar with the equipment or even sewing leather? Completing one strap wasn't enough to make her an expert. He didn't want to hurt her feelings, but he would be better off if she stayed with her sisters. She would be better off, too.

He shook his head. "I understand you want to repay me in some way. It isn't necessary. It's kind of you to offer, but you are here to enjoy a visit, not to work."

Disappointment flashed in her eyes and then something that looked like defiance.

Her chin went up a notch. "You think I can't do it?"

He sought to smooth over the moment. "I'm sure you could if someone taught you."

"You can teach me."

He glanced around again. "I wouldn't know where to start. There's a lot more to harness making and leatherwork than simple sewing. It isn't like making a dress."

She crossed her arms. "Have you made many dresses?"

He shifted uncomfortably from one foot to the other. "*Nee*, I haven't."

"Then you don't know if the skill required is similar or not. I'm not offering to make a complete harness. I have no idea how to operate your equipment. I'm offering to stitch and perhaps embellish some of your smaller items."

He stared at her intently. What was behind this offer? "Why?"

She held out her hands and gestured around the room. "This would keep me from becoming bored while I'm here. I like to sew."

Or was it her way of trying to ingratiate herself to him? She might say she didn't want a hearing husband, but she hadn't come all the way to Maine to view the wildlife. He didn't like the feeling that he and his brothers were on Waneta's shopping list. It made him suspicious.

The outside door opened, and Waneta stepped in. "There you are, Jonah. I need your help with something. Come along."

"But I'm signing for Gabe," the boy said.

Waneta sent Gabe a knowing smile. "I'm sure he can make himself understood. Esther reads lips better than she lets on. Don't make me wait." Waneta held the door open. Jonah sighed heavily but went out with her.

When the door closed, Gabe looked at Esther. She was still staring at the door. He hesitated, then touched her arm. She glanced at him. "Do you?" he asked.

"Do I what?"

"Speech-read better than you let on?"

"Is that what she said?" Anger flashed in her eyes before she schooled her features into the appearance of calmness. She did it so easily he wondered how often she was forced to practice the move. He admired her self-control.

She kept her gaze fastened to his. "I didn't know she had come in. I wasn't looking toward her until I noticed Jonah staring behind me. All I caught was 'Don't make me wait.' I have no idea what she said before that."

"That has to be frustrating, only catching part of a conversation because you happen to look away or don't see someone behind you."

She tipped her head slightly as she regarded him. "It is. Few people make that connection unless they are used to being around a deaf person who lip-reads."

"I don't know any deaf people personally. It just seems logical."

Her eyes sparkled as a slight smile curved her lips. "You would think so, but not everyone is as observant as you are."

He wanted to ask her why she hadn't taken the information about the hearing device yesterday but thought better of it. It wasn't any of his business. He needed to get to work, not stand here wasting time visiting with Esther, no matter how interesting she was turning out to be.

"About my offer?" she prompted.

"I appreciate it, but I think not." He hoped he wasn't going to wound her, but she deserved his honesty. "I don't have the time to teach you what you would need to know."

Her expressive face went blank. "I should go back to the house." She hurried to the door.

He had hurt her feelings. "Esther, wait. I'm sorry."

She left the shop without looking back. Of course she didn't turn around. She couldn't hear him.

He stood staring at the door for several seconds. He could chase after her and apologize, but maybe this was for the best.

He picked up a length of leather and fed it into his shiver to cut down the thickness of the piece. When he was done, he added it to the pile of belts on the table waiting to be stitched. Working the shiver to decrease the thickness of the leather didn't pull his stitches the way trying to operate the sewing machine did. He would cut out as many pieces as he could and do the sewing when his arm was better in a day or two. He hoped.

A little past noon, the door opened. His father looked in. "Gideon Beachy's feed wagon has a busted axle and broken rear wheel. It will take all of us to get it repaired before he has to feed his dairy cows again this evening. Seth has gone into Fort Craig to see about some scrap iron for sale."

Gabe laid aside the leather stip. "I thought I'd get some work in here done today, but reckon I thought wrong."

"I'm sorry, *sohn*. I can't neglect a paying job or our neighbor. I need you."

"Of course." Gabe laid the last strip of leather on the pile, grabbed his hat and followed his father. As he climbed on the wagon with his brothers, he caught sight of Esther in the garden with her brother. He should have taken her up on her offer. She could have stitched a belt or two for him while he was gone. He nodded to her. She pointedly looked away. It didn't appear that she would be willing to help him in the future. He resigned himself to another lost day of work.

"Where are Zeke and his sons going?" Esther asked Jonah, who was helping her weed Talitha's garden.

He shook his head, not bothering to sign. Esther stared at Gabe's empty workshop. He didn't think she had the skill required to stitch a few simple straight lines. That was basically all the belts and dog leashes required. Unless he wanted to produce fancier pieces. She was quite capable of stitching a zigzag if that were the case.

She resumed hoeing the weeds with renewed vigor. Being deaf didn't make her incapable of learning. Unfortunately some people assumed that it did. She would love to prove him wrong.

She stopped hoeing. She shouldn't be this annoyed. Why was she?

Because she'd had a few glimpses of empathy from Gabe Fisher. She thought he was different.

Jonah tapped the handle of the hoe she was leaning on and signed, "Maybe Pamela knows."

Esther looked toward the house and saw Pamela walking toward her with a bowl in her hands. She stopped at the first row of green beans, squatted down and began searching among the leaves for pods that were big enough to pluck.

"Where did the Fisher men go?" Esther asked.

Pamela looked up. "To help a neighbor with a broken wagon."

Esther glanced at the workshop again. "Will they be gone long?" She looked at her sister to see the answer.

"I heard Zeke say they wouldn't be back for several hours."

Several hours. How much stitching could she get done before Gabe returned? Enough to prove that she was capable of doing more? Would he be angry if she invaded his workspace without him? Was it worth risking his ire just to show him he was wrong about her usefulness?

Maybe it was.

She resumed hoeing. As soon as she finished this task, she was going to take another look around Gabe's workshop. If there happened to be something that she could sew for him, she would. If there wasn't anything cut, she wouldn't risk ruining one of his pieces of leather. She'd just leave, close the door and pretend she had never gone back. She began to hoe more quickly.

Fifteen minutes later she put her gardening tool back in the shed and hurried around the side of the house before Waneta noticed she was done with her chore. If Waneta saw Esther wasn't busy, she always found something for her to do. At the door to Gabe's shop, Esther glanced around to make sure no one was looking for her and then she slipped inside.

The wonderful smells of leather and tanning oil made her smile. Perhaps she couldn't hear the sounds of the world, but there was nothing wrong with her nose. She took delight in the different fragrances of life and the way the scent of something could bring a treasured memory into sharp focus. Only now she needed to concentrate on finding what work, if any, she could do for Gabe.

There were tanned hides stacked in one corner of the room waiting to be cut into usable shapes. Some of the leather was thick and black. Other pieces were thinner, more supple and dyed different shades of brown. There was little she could do with the uncut pieces. She turned her attention to the other side of the room and saw a stack of leather cut into strips of varying lengths but all exactly the same width. Unless she was badly mistaken, these were for belts. She grabbed the top three and carried them to Gabe's sewing machine.

There were several spools of colored thread to choose from, but she decided to go with the creamy color that was already on the machine that Gabe had set up earlier. She looked back over her shoulder at the closed door.

She could put back the strips and leave. He would never know she had been inside without his knowledge. A quick retreat was tempting. She focused on the machine again. Proving him wrong was even more of a temptation.

After she stitched five of the belts with the creamy thread, her eyes were drawn to the spool of red thread. It would look pretty against the black leather. It took her a few minutes to figure out how to re-thread the machine. When she was done, she set the needle for the first stitch and stared at the belt. What if she made a series of Xs instead of doing a straight stitch? How would that look? She pictured it in her mind's eye. It certainly wouldn't be plain. Would customers like it?

The more important question was, what would Gabe think of such a design? If she went ahead and he didn't like it, the leather would be ruined.

She took a deep breath and began to sew. With each pull of the lever, she ad-justed the angle of the strap and soon had a row of Xs almost done when light spilled in, brightening the room. She knew the outside door had been opened.

She turned around slowly. Gabe was standing in the doorway with a frightening scowl on his face and one hand clamped over his injured arm. She kept her chin up with difficulty as she focused on his mouth. She didn't want to miss what he had to say.

He stood there for a long moment before he stepped into the room. His eyes moved from her to the stack of leather belts on the table beside the sewing machine. He didn't say anything. He walked over and picked up one of the belts. He turned so he could examine it in the brighter light.

Still without speaking he spread the others out, looking carefully at each one. Then he noticed the piece still on the machine. One eyebrow shot up and he looked directly at her. "Interesting."

While it wasn't praise, it certainly wasn't condemnation. "I thought so."

His gaze roved over the room. She sat up straighter. "I didn't touch any of your equipment other than the sewing machine."

He nodded and then walked to the piles of leather. He withdrew one from a smaller stack and walked to the cutting table. He continued to hold his injured arm tight against his chest. She thought he said something but couldn't tell for sure. He sent her a questioning look over his shoulder.

She crossed her arms. "What?"

"Sorry. I asked if you wanted to learn how to cut patterns. I'll show you what templates I have. You can finish that piece later."

"You aren't angry with me?"

He cocked his head to the side. "Why should I be angry?"

"You were when you opened the door and saw me in here."

"*Nee*, it was not an angry expression you saw. It was only discomfort."

"Your arm is paining you?"

"Some. How is your head?"

She unfolded her arms and settled her hands on her hips. "Do you want the truth?"

"Certainly."

"Throbbing, but not as bad as yesterday. Now tell me again, how is your arm?"

He cradled it with his good hand and

grinned. "Stinging and aching something fierce. I think I may have torn a stitch."

She looked at him, aghast. "Did you just say you might have torn your stitches?"

He sobered. "That's what I said. Am I hard to understand?"

"I get most of what you are saying. I can guess at the rest. I'm just shocked that you came in here to work. March up to the house and let me take a look at your arm. You will need a new bandage, anyway. It has bled through onto your shirtsleeve." She pointed to the door. "Now. Go. Did you understand that?"

"I got it." He walked to the door and held it open for her.

Her shoulder brushed against him as she walked past. She sucked in a quick breath as the contact sent her pulse racing. Why did he have such a strange effect on her?

She smelled like a garden in the sunshine. It wasn't something Gabe had expected to encounter in his workshop. Perhaps she used a shampoo with a floral scent that lingered, or maybe it was simply her.

She was a breath of fresh air. More direct than any woman he knew except his mother. He liked her. But she wouldn't be here long, and she wasn't interested in a walking out with a fellow like him. He'd never thought having good hearing would be a drawback in a relationship, but it was in her case. Not that he had the time or the inclination to court a woman this summer. He didn't. He had work to do.

At the house his father was seated at the kitchen table with a cup of coffee in his hand as he waited for supper. Esther pointed to a chair. "Sit. Roll up your sleeve."

Esther gently unwound the bandage. His mother and Waneta came in from his mother's quilting room. "What has happened?" his mother asked.

"I tore a stitch loose. It's nothing. Esther is taking care of it."

Waneta called for Julia, who came in from the other room. "See to Gabe's arm.

Julia has taken first-aid training and helps our local volunteer fire department," she explained as she drew Esther aside.

"Esther was doing fine," he said, watching her retreat to the living room.

His mother scowled in disapproval at his father. "You told me the doctor said he wasn't to use his arm for a week."

"I told the boy not to lift with that arm, didn't I, Gabe?"

"You did, but it couldn't be helped. We got the wagon fixed. That's what counts." Gabe hissed as Julia cleaned the rest of the stitches with peroxide.

"You will have to watch for any signs of infection," she said, stepping back. "I'll change the dressing again tomorrow."

"*Danki.* Am I free to go?"

Julia nodded. Waneta beamed at her, then looked at Gabe. "Julia is calm and capable in an emergency. Wonderful traits for a wife to have, don't you think?"

"I reckon so." He stood, rolled down his sleeve and went into the living room. Esther was seated by the window staring outside. Her hands were clenched into fists on her lap. Jonah stood nearby with a scowl on his face.

Gabe crossed the room to stand beside Esther. She looked up at him. He nodded toward the front door. "We have work to do."

Her eyes widened in surprise. She grinned and jumped to her feet. "I'm ready if you are."

"Then come on. Jonah, I may need your help." Gabe led the way through the kitchen and out the door.

Jonah hurried to keep up with him. "Gladly, but can we go look for a moose later? I've been hoping to see one."

"Did your sister tell you about the one we saw this morning?"

"*Nee*, she did not." Jonah touched Esther's arm and signed quickly.

Esther signed back, ruffled his hair and went into the workshop.

"What did she say?" Gabe asked.

"She said if I get up early I might be

able to see him tomorrow. Do you think he'll return?"

"They tend to feed in one area for several days. It's possible."

Inside the workroom, Gabe went to his cutting table and pulled out several of the templates he had made for cutting out holsters, knife sheaths and wallets. Jonah was able to convey his instructions to Esther as Gabe had to keep his eyes on what he was cutting so he didn't ruin a piece of leather. Esther watched and asked pointed questions about the properties of the leather he chose for each item. She had a quick mind, and she didn't waste time with chitchat.

When Gabe had enough items cut out to keep her busy stitching for the rest of the day, he sent Jonah back to the house and turned his attention to making the pony-size harness that Willis Gingrich, the local Amish blacksmith, had ordered. He was cutting the driving lines an hour later when he noticed the sewing machine had stopped. He looked over to see Esther rubbing her temples with both hands.

She glanced his way. "I'm done."

He shouldn't have put her to work so soon. "That's fine. Go to the house and rest. I will finish them tomorrow."

"I mean I'm done with what you gave me. Do you trust me to cut out more?"

He made his way to her side. The neatly stitched items were stacked together on a table beside her chair. He picked up several of the wallets, knowing they took the most work, and examined them closely. The stitching was flawless. He shook his head in disbelief.

Worry filled her eyes. "Is something wrong? Did I make a mistake?"

"*Nee*, your work is every bit as good as I could have done, and you did it in a quarter of the time it would have taken me. To think I wondered how much help you could possibly be."

Her eyes narrowed. "Because I'm deaf?"

"Because you said you hadn't used a machine like mine or worked in leather before." He held out the wallet. "Tell me the truth. Do you do this at home?"

She laughed. "I do not, but it's easier than making a dress or a shirt. I can do more if you will cut some for me."

"Not now. I want you to go rest. Your headache is worse."

"How do you know that?"

"I can see it in your eyes."

She rubbed her temples. "I said you were observant. Very well, I will go lie down for a bit."

He watched her leave and then looked at the work they had gotten done in one morning. With Esther's help, he could finish more than enough pieces in the next three weeks to sell at the upcoming festival. His hopes rose for the first time in ages. His plan just might work.

# Chapter Five

Esther only meant to lie down for half an hour or so, but when she woke, she realized she had been asleep for over four hours. It was too late to go back to Gabe's shop. She sat up and discovered her headache was almost gone.

Nancy was sitting on a chair nearby. "Feeling better?" she signed.

Esther grinned. "Much better."

"Gabe was concerned when you didn't come down for supper."

"I promised to help him in his workshop. He must think I deserted him."

Nancy shook her head and signed, "He

said you were not to do any more work for him today."

"Oh." Esther was surprised at the sharpness of her disappointment. Had he decided he could get along better without her?

"He said rest and tomorrow will be soon enough to get started again."

Relief made Esther smile. "That's *wunderbar*. I'm happy to help him. I owe him so much."

"He seems like a nice fellow. Waneta certainly thinks so."

"I do, too. What about you? Have any of the brothers caught your eye?"

"After a day? I hardly think so. You sound like Waneta. She asked us all that very question this morning. Why is she so set on having us marry?"

Esther had wondered the same thing. "Perhaps she wants our father all to herself."

"She won't have that until Jonah marries, and he is only ten. Are you ready to go downstairs?"

"I am. I'm starving."

"I'm sure Talitha can find you something. A soup bone to gnaw on or a crust of bread."

Esther gave her sister a playful shove. "I'm sure our hostess has more than that laid by for her guests."

"You wouldn't be so sure if you saw how much food her sons eat. Moses must still be growing. He ate more than any of them."

"Then someone should point out that you are the best cook among us, little sister," Esther said, holding back a grin.

Nancy stuck out her tongue and signed, "I expect Waneta will get around to mentioning it soon enough. We are working on a quilt in Talitha's sewing room. Will you join us?"

"I think not. It's difficult to quilt and gossip if you must stop and sign everything for me. You go and join the fun. I think I'll have a bite to eat and go back to sleep. I can't believe how tired I am."

"You are trying to do too much too fast."

"Maybe you're right."

The sisters walked downstairs together. Esther discovered that Talitha had left a plate of roast beef, carrots and potatoes warming in the oven for her. She enjoyed her solitary meal and then went back to bed.

The following morning she came down to breakfast to find everyone had already finished. She stepped outside and paused on the steps, wondering what she should do, when she caught sight of Gabe coming out of his workshop just as his brother Seth came out of the barn. Gabe must have called out to his brother, because Seth stopped, nodded and then continued his way. Gabe walked toward her. He held a pair of bridles in his hand.

He paused in front of her with his eyes focused on her face. "Are you feeling better?"

"Much. I'm ready to do more sewing for you."

He shook his head. "Not right now. How about a walk in the fresh air?"

She sighed. "I know you have work that needs doing. You don't have to babysit me."

He grinned and held up the bridles. "Didn't you hear me tell Seth just now that I'm walking over to the Arnett farm to deliver these?"

His grin vanished. He flushed a deep red. "You couldn't have heard that. I'm sorry. That was an inconsiderate thing to say."

"Don't be sorry, Gabe. You haven't offended me. I am as I am."

Esther could see he was still uncomfortable. He shifted from one foot to the other. "Mrs. Arnett is our neighbor. Her place isn't far. It's a pleasant walk through the woods. Would you care to join me?"

She didn't want him to worry that something he said or did would upset her. "I would like that. *Danki.* You realize you will have to walk backward most of the way so that I can see what you're saying to me."

She tried not to smile, but she couldn't

help it. The look of puzzled confusion on his face was priceless. She burst out laughing.

It quickly dawned on Gabe that Esther was teasing him. Was she joking about her condition to put him at ease? It was a generous move. "Laughing at the man who saved your life isn't the nicest way to repay him."

"What would be a better way?"

"If you could forgive his fumbling words."

"You are forgiven, as long as you promise not to treat me differently from my sisters or your other friends."

"I'll try my best. This way." He nodded toward the barn.

"Let me get something first."

She rushed back inside and soon returned with a blue quilted bag slung over her shoulder. "I'm ready."

"The path through the woods is just beyond the barn. If I have anything important to say while we are walking, I'll make sure I get your attention first."

"That sounds like a sound plan. If you hear of a better one, you should give me a shout." She arched her brow. "Get it?"

He rolled his eyes. "I get it. I'm free to use words that refer to hearing. You won't be offended."

"Excellent. I like the sound of that." Her wide grin made him smile, too.

"Enough. I'm going. Tag along if you like." He started toward the path. She quickly fell into step beside him. Less than a hundred yards beyond the barn, they entered a grove of pine trees. The path skirted around moss-covered boulders thrust up through the earth and skeletons of old fallen pine trees. The dappled sunlight was broken in places by openings in the canopy that allowed the brightness to reach the forest floor. Those spaces were filled with shrubs, plants and young trees eager to take advantage of the light.

The air was filled with birdsongs and the sighing of the wind in the branches overhead. Gabe kept alert for the sounds or glimpses of animals. There were black bears in the area as well as moose. It wouldn't do to surprise either one of them.

They skirted the edge of a shallow pond when suddenly Esther stopped. "Oh, how pretty."

Gabe turned to see her crouched beside a cluster of small blue flowers. She looked up at him. "What are these called?"

"I don't know." He pointed overhead. "But that is a Harris's sparrow. A rare bird in these parts."

She stood and moved closer to him. "Did you say a rare bird? Where?"

"Near the top of that spruce." She looked where he was pointing.

"He's kind of streaky brown and black. He has a black bib, a black face and a small black crown." Gabe stopped talking when he realized she wasn't looking at him. She couldn't hear the bird's call or his description.

"Is it that black-and-brown bird with a

little black hat on his head?" She turned to look at Gabe.

He nodded. "That's the one."

"He's pretty, but I like flowers better. Are you a bird-watcher?"

"I am. I keep a record of the rare ones that I see."

She knelt beside the flowers again. "I keep pressed petals in an album. I like to sketch them in their native setting, too. I wish I knew the name of this one."

He touched her arm to get her attention. "Take a sprig. Mrs. Arnett might know. She's a Maine native."

"I hate to disturb the plant until I know it's a common species. I'd like to make a quick sketch instead if you don't mind."

He had work waiting but he couldn't deny her this simple joy. "Go ahead."

*"Danki."* She opened her satchel and pulled out a pad along with some colored pencils.

He moved a few feet away and took a seat on a fallen log to watch her. She bent close to the flowers, looking at them from several angles before she settled on the ground, opened her book and started drawing.

She seemed at home in the woods. The patterns of sunlight filtering down on her made her blend into the surroundings, for her dress was nearly the same shade of blue as the flowers at her feet. She chewed the tip of her pencil as she regarded her subject before bending over the paper once more.

He heard a rustling in the leaves behind him and scanned the woods for the source of the sound. A gray squirrel scampered up a nearby tree and chittered loudly from a dead branch.

"What are you looking at?" Esther asked.

"That squirrel. He's upset with us." He glanced at her and realized she was still waiting for his answer. How long would it take him to learn he had to be looking at her before he spoke? It wasn't as easy as it sounded.

"A squirrel is scolding us. Are you finished?"

"I am."

"May I see it?" He held out his hand.

She hesitated then handed over her sketch pad. She had captured the size, color and even the texture of the plant. "The Lord has given you quite a talent."

She took the picture away from him. "I think flowers are easy to draw."

"Not for me they aren't. I tend to avoid floral designs on my tooled leatherwork for that reason."

"Perhaps I can give you some pointers when I get back to work."

"I look forward to it," he said and realized he meant it. She was an intriguing woman. He found he wanted to know her better.

They started along the path again, but it wasn't long before she stopped to examine another cluster of blooms. "What are these?"

"I haven't a clue."

"Oh." She walked on but soon stopped

beside a group of miniature daisylike blossoms. "These are lovely. Do you know what they're called?"

"Weeds."

She shot him a sour look. "Weeds or not, they're pretty."

"At this rate we won't get to the Arnett farm before dark."

"Okay, I'll stop looking at the flowers."

"Weeds."

Her eyes flashed with annoyance. "I refuse to call something with such delicate petals and this sweet scent a weed."

She walked off ahead of him, so she didn't see his grin. She might pretend to be annoyed with him, but he could tell she wasn't. He was discovering that Esther Burkholder was a very interesting woman even if Waneta had brought her here on a husband-hunting mission.

The thought drew him up short. He wasn't in the market for a wife. He had to keep his focus on improving the family's precarious financial situation.

\* \* \*

Esther was sorry when the woods opened suddenly into a field until she realized she was walking out amid acres of blossoming potato plants. The air was filled with their delicate fragrance as the white flowers atop the bright green foliage trembled in the breeze. Gabe came up beside her and gestured around them. "Not weeds," he said when he was sure she was looking at him.

She rolled her eyes. "Are you trying to be funny?"

"I am. Did it work?"

She chuckled. "I'm mildly amused."

"I'm usually much funnier."

"I can hardly wait to see a sample. Is that where we're going?" She pointed toward a farmstead a few hundred yards away.

"Yup."

Together they walked toward the farm. An *Englisch* woman wearing jeans and a red plaid shirt came out of the barn carrying a bucket. She caught sight of them and waved.

Gabe waved back. The woman put her bucket down and came to greet them. "Hello, Gabe. I see you have my bridles. Who is this with you?"

Gabe looked at Esther. "Esther, this is Lilly Arnett. She farms here by herself. Lilly, this is Esther Burkholder. She and her family are visiting from Ohio. Esther is Deaf but can speech-read or read lips, as they sometimes say. You must be looking at her when you speak. She is also a wildflower lover. Perhaps you can identify one she sketched."

Lilly held out her hand. "I'm pleased to meet you. I'd be happy to look at your drawing."

Esther pulled her sketchbook from her bag and opened it before handing it to Lilly. "I think it must be a violet of some sort."

"It's a New England violet. They are rare. Where did you find it?"

"Alongside a small pond just off the path that leads here."

Lilly smiled. "They do like moist ground. I may go gather some seeds and plant a few in my wildflower garden. You must come and see it. It's my pride and joy."

Esther happily followed Lilly to an area at the side of her house, where a stepping-stone path led down to a small stream. A profusion of flowers graced the gentle slope in a multitude of colors and sizes, from small bleeding hearts clustered beside the path to tall nodding white yarrow, blue spires of lupine and everything in between. A stone bench stood beneath the spreading branches of an oak tree that overlooked the area. Esther's fingers itched to get out her pencils and paper.

She grinned at Lilly. "It's beautiful."

"Thank you. I feel close to God when I come down here to just sit and admire His handiwork."

"I know what you mean." Esther, too,

felt close to God when she was in her flower garden at home.

Gabe handed Lilly the bridles. "I hope these are what you wanted."

"Let's see." She led the way to a corral where two horses stood. She opened the gate and slipped a bridle on one of them. Both she and Gabe checked the fit, and Lilly seemed satisfied. The two of them spoke briefly, but Esther couldn't see what they were saying. When Gabe returned to her side, she waved goodbye to Lilly and waited for him to speak.

"I invited Lilly to the picnic. I hope you don't mind. I thought you might enjoy visiting with someone who shares your hobby. She'd like to see more of your sketches."

It was kind of him to invite someone she knew and would have something in common with. Large groups weren't comfortable for her unless she was with people who could sign. Her sisters often performed that service, but with Waneta insisting they focus on finding mates, Esther wasn't sure they would have time for her.

"I'll be happy to show Lilly my drawings at the gathering. Have you decided to go to the picnic?"

"If we get enough work done this afternoon and tomorrow, I might."

Esther smiled, amazed at how happy it made her to know he could be coming. "*Goot.* Then I'll sew up a storm."

Gabe was busy in his workshop early the following morning when Esther came in. He had a dozen leather knife sheaths tooled with a basket-weave pattern ready to be assembled. "I didn't expect you until after breakfast."

"I wanted to get an early start to make up for our lost time yesterday morning," she said, moving to take a seat.

"We made up for most of that in the afternoon. I'm nearly caught up."

It didn't take long for him to show her what he wanted done. After that they worked in silence with only the sound of his mallet tapping designs into leather pieces and the steady thumping of the sewing machine. He glanced over several times to make sure she wasn't having trouble. Once she looked up and caught his eye. She frowned slightly. "Did you say something?"

He shook his head, and she went back to work. After an hour he heard his mother calling him. Gabe put his tools aside and touched Esther's shoulder. When she looked up, he nodded toward the door. "Breakfast is ready."

"I'll be in as soon as I finish this piece." She went back to pulling the lever on the stitcher.

He pulled her chair back. She frowned at him. "What are you doing?"

"Finish after we eat. Our families will be waiting on us."

A mutinous expression crossed her face but quickly disappeared. "Very well."

He followed her out the door and across the farmyard to the house. Inside, his brothers and Jonah were lined up on one side of the table while her sisters and Waneta were seated across from them. His father sat at the head of the table. His mother filled all the cups with coffee, returned the pot to the stove and took her place at the foot of the table. Everyone bowed their heads for a silent blessing.

There was very little conversation until everyone was finished eating. Jonah, seated opposite Esther, signed for her when needed.

Gabe's father cleared his throat. "We have a broken spring on the bishop's buggy to repair today. Seth, you and Asher can manage that. I want to get a few more spare buggy wheels built so we have a ready supply when one is needed. Moses, do you have anything going on?"

"*Nee*, I'm free to help you."

"*Goot*. Waneta, what are you and the girls going to do today?"

"We are almost finished with Talitha's quilt. After that we'll bake a few things for the picnic tomorrow. Nancy works in a bakery in our town. She's very skilled, as

I'm sure you will agree when you sample her creations tomorrow."

Nancy signed something for Esther, who smothered a laugh. Waneta scowled at them.

"Esther will be helping me today," Gabe said quickly.

His mother took a sip of her coffee and put her cup down. "I hope you aren't taking advantage of her kindness in offering to sew for you?"

"He isn't," Esther said. "I enjoy it. I'm hoping he will show me how to tool some of the pieces, too." She picked up her plate and began to clear the table. Her sisters quickly joined her. Gabe waited outside for Esther to join him. When she came out, he smiled at her. "Would you really like to learn to tool leather?"

"I would."

"Once we finish the pieces I already have cut, I'll show you the basic tools I use. Does that sound okay to you?"

She smiled broadly, proving she recalled

their conversation yesterday. "You are a quick learner."

"I try."

They entered the workshop and spent the rest of the morning concentrating on their own tasks as the finished pieces piled up. He looked at the growing stack. With Esther's help over the next two weeks, he would have plenty of items to sell.

It was almost noon when the outside door opened. Waneta came in, followed by Pamela.

"I see Esther is still taking up all your time, Gabriel," Waneta said. "You don't have to continue to indulge her."

"I'm not humoring her," he said with a pointed look at Waneta. "She is a skilled worker."

Waneta ignored his rebuke. "Why don't you show Pamela some of your work? She is interested in leatherworking, too. Pamela, tell Esther Talitha would like her to work on the quilt with us for a while and then I have some errands I need her to run." She turned around and left.

Gabe watched the exchange take place in sign language. Esther wasn't pleased. She shot an angry look toward the door but got up and allowed Pamela to sit down. Esther glanced at Gabe. "I'm sorry, but I have to go."

"That's okay. Pamela can help me."

Pamela looked the sewing machine up and down. "I'm not too sure about that."

He spent the next hour teaching Pamela the basics of stitching leather while his own work went by the wayside. She had dozens of questions, which he answered patiently, but she didn't possess the skills Esther had. He was glad when they had to go in for lunch.

Waneta and Nancy served up the meal. He didn't see his mother or Esther. He turned to his father. "Where is *Mamm*?"

"She went into Fort Craig to pick up some material for a new dress."

"And Esther?" Gabe looked at Waneta.

"I sent her along to keep your mother company and to buy some things I need.

I'm sure Pamela can help you again this afternoon."

"I'm not really much help," Pamela admitted. "My talents lie more with quilting."

"I see," Waneta said with a tight smile. "Nancy, perhaps you would like to give Gabe a hand."

"I guess I could," Nancy said.

She clearly wasn't eager to do so, and Gabe wasn't eager to waste more time teaching a reluctant pupil. "I have harness cutting work to do this afternoon. I don't need help with that." He concentrated on the meat loaf and mashed potatoes on his plate, but his appetite was gone. It looked like he'd miss the picnic tomorrow after all.

Was Waneta suddenly intent on keeping Esther away from him? If so, why?

## *Chapter Six*

**W**hen Esther returned from town with Gabe's mother, she found Pamela and Nancy in the kitchen rolling out pie dough. Talitha was putting away the horse and buggy.

Esther laid the packages her stepmother wanted on the table. "Waneta, I have your things. Pamela, I thought you were helping Gabe."

Pamela put aside her rolling pin and looked at Esther. "He said he needed to work alone on cutting a harness." She glanced at Waneta, who was slicing apples and signed, "I don't think I was much help, anyway. I'm sorry she made you leave."

"That's okay. It wasn't your fault," **Esther** signed. She cleared her throat. "Gabe was going to show me how to decorate leather with stamping and tooling. I think I'll go see if he has time now."

Waneta turned around. "You shouldn't monopolize his time, Esther. You've made no secret of the fact that you won't consider marrying someone who isn't deaf. Give your sisters a chance to get to know Gabriel. One of them may suit him. How will they find out if he is constantly with you?"

"It won't be me," **Pamela** signed then transferred the pie dough into a pan and crimped the edges.

Waneta scowled at her then looked at Esther. "I've decided you may return to Ohio with Bessie. I walked to the phone booth today and called her. She said she'd be happy to have your company on the return trip."

It was what Esther had wanted, so why

wasn't she happier about the prospect? Because Gabe needed her help and she liked helping him. "Did *Daed* agree to this? He wanted me to come."

"And we both know why. I'll write and tell him tomorrow. I'm sure he won't object when I explain."

"When is Bessie coming back?"

"In ten days. Take over on these apples, Esther." Waneta left the kitchen with her packages. Esther hadn't agreed to go, but she knew she had little chance of changing Waneta's mind when it was made up.

Esther grabbed the paring knife and began peeling the bright red fruit. Maybe it would be best if she did leave. She hadn't been trying to prevent her sisters from getting to know Gabe. She only wanted to repay him for his kindness. She was a little amazed that she enjoyed fashioning leather pieces as much as she did. In fact she had a few ideas for new items for him to sell.

She had seen several leather purses for sale in Fort Craig and realized Gabe didn't have any among the items he'd made. He had men's wallets and men's belts but nothing specifically for women customers. She was eager to suggest he add some and see what he thought of the idea. She even had several sketches to show him.

Now she wouldn't get to see how well his booth did at the festival. She would be going home before then.

She drew a deep breath. She had ten days left. She would show Gabe her drawings and see if he liked the idea, and then she'd find a way to help him make them. If she worked hard enough, she might manage to stitch all the items he would need for the festival.

An Amish man from a neighboring community arrived after supper to inquire about a new buggy for his son who was getting married. Zeke and his sons spent the evening going over plans, helping the man choose interior fabric and seat covers and then settling on the price in the living room. Esther didn't get a chance to speak to Gabe alone.

After supper the women set to baking cakes, cookies and pies that would be taken to the picnic along with a large ham, fried chicken, potato salad and fresh vegetables from the garden. As Esther was helping clean up the kitchen afterward, Talitha touched her arm.

"Are you feeling well enough to go with us tomorrow? The gathering is at noon."

Esther grinned and nodded. "I'm looking forward to it. Gabe introduced me to Lilly Arnett. It seems we share a love of wildflowers. She is coming, so I will know someone besides your family. I still have a slight headache, but I barely notice it most of the time."

Talitha turned toward the living room. Esther looked that way and saw Gabe standing in the doorway. He nodded toward her, but there was an odd wariness in his eyes.

"I'm glad you're feeling good enough to go. Lilly is looking forward to seeing your flower sketches. I wish I could go," he said and looked at his feet.

Esther frowned. He wasn't coming? "I thought you were going to join us? You said you could afford to take the day off."

"I've fallen further behind in my work. I need to do some catching up."

"That's a shame." Her anticipation faded away. She hadn't been eager to go until Gabe said he was going.

"He needs a day away from that shop," Talitha said to Esther. "He takes on too much." She walked past him and left the room.

"I'm sorry you're behind in your work." Esther sucked in a quick breath when she noticed a stain on his shirt. "Gabe, there's blood on your sleeve again."

"I overused my arm trying to stitch. It's nothing."

"I thought Pamela was helping you."

He shook his head ruefully. "She doesn't have your skill at leatherwork." He took a step closer. "Did I upset you? Is that why you didn't come back this afternoon?"

"*Nee*, my stepmother had errands for me

to run in town. They took longer than I thought they would."

"I hoped it wasn't something I said or did."

She gazed at him quizzically. "Why would you think that?"

"Jonah said only about half our words can be understood by a person reading lips. Sometimes I forget to look at you when I speak, or I look away when I'm talking. I was worried that you didn't understand how much I appreciate your help."

Esther decided he needed to know the truth. "My stepmother doesn't want me taking up all your time."

"You're not. How can she think that?"

Esther swallowed hard. "She wants you to have a chance to get to know my sisters better."

Comprehension dawned on him. "Because they are hoping to find a husband here and you are not?"

She nodded. It sounded so cold when he put it that way.

His brow furrowed as he shook his head in disgust and threw his hands up. "I don't have the—courting someone." She missed part of what he said when he looked down.

"My work must come first. This family has—on—my success. Your sisters will—with brothers—fellows they'll meet at the picnic tomorrow. Single women— in New Covenant. They'll—sought after, I'm sure."

Esther stood quietly waiting for him to finish.

The scowl left his face. He took another step closer. "I'm sorry to rant at you. Did you understand all that I said?"

"I think so. You don't want to court anyone. My sisters can look elsewhere."

A wry grin tipped up the corner of his mouth. "That's about it."

"I can understand you fairly well. You're one of the rare people I find easy to read. For the most part you speak slowly and distinctly, and you have an expressive face, but if you look down or away from me, I miss things. Reconsider and come to the picnic. It will do you good and give your arm a chance to heal."

He stepped back. "I wish I could. I'll see you in the morning. *Guten nacht*, Esther."

"Good night, Gabe."

He turned and walked away.

Esther leaned on the table with both arms. She didn't want to go to the picnic if he wasn't coming. He needed to come. Even his mother thought so. Esther pushed away from the table and walked toward the stairs. How could she convince him to change his mind?

Gabe rose before first light, grabbed a cold biscuit from the bread box and washed it down with a glass of milk. If he got started early and worked through the morning, he might be able to spare an hour to attend the picnic. He wanted Esther to meet his friends. He wanted to see her enjoying herself.

Opening the front door, he paused when he noticed a light coming from the window of his workshop. He distinctly remembered turning off the overhead propane lamp when he left the building yesterday. Who had business out there at this hour?

He hurried across the farmyard and opened the door. An Amish woman sat at his stitching machine. He knew it was Esther without seeing her face. He walked up behind her. She raised her head. "Good morning, Gabe." She turned around with a smile.

"How did you know I was here?"

"I felt the vibration of someone walking across the floor. I assumed it was you."

"What are you doing?"

"I'm stitching the pieces I didn't get done yesterday."

"How long have you been out here?"

"About two hours. I have at least another hour of work to do. Hadn't you better get busy? We don't want to be late to the picnic today."

"I said I wasn't going."

"And I'm helping you catch up on your work so you can. You mother said you need a day off. I agree with her, and you should do as your mother bids."

"I don't stand a chance of getting my own way if you've teamed up with *Mamm*."

She frowned. "Say that again but slower."

He repeated himself, and she chuckled. "Very smart of you to recognize that. I'm almost done with what I have here. What's next?"

"Dog collars and leashes. I cut. You stitch."

She grinned. "Easy straight lines. What color thread are you wanting?"

"What do you think?"

"Mostly red, but I would do a few in blue and a few in pink."

"Pink? For a dog collar?"

"*Englisch* women like their dogs to wear fancy things. I saw pink collars with rhinestones on several little dogs in town yesterday."

"I don't have any rhinestones."

"You do have brass and chrome dots in

round and diamond shapes. You even have little brass bells. I checked. Plain items are all good and well for your Amish customers, but the *Englisch* like fancy."

He rubbed his jaw as he considered her suggestion. She could be right. Only a handful of the festivalgoers would be Amish, but over half of the rest would be women. "What else might an *Englisch* woman want to buy from us?"

"Not ax and hatchet covers."

"There are plenty of lumberjacks in this part of Maine, and they like to protect their tools."

"Women lumberjacks?"

"Some."

She arched one eyebrow and gave him a skeptical look.

"Okay, not many."

"Women like bags and purses, pretty belts, soft leather baby boots, perhaps."

It was his turn to be dubious. "Plain bags and plain purses?"

He saw her take a deep breath. "Some plain, but some with fancy designs in the leather. Flowers, leaves, feathers, vines, and the inside of the purses would need to be lined with fabric. I've made several sketches." She slowly handed over her drawing pad.

The shapes of the bags themselves were simple enough, but her elaborate designs would take hours to complete on each piece. "Fabric? Flowers? I thought your plan was to help me so I had less work to do, not more."

"You're right. I'm sorry." She reached for her sketches.

He held them away from her and carried them over to his workbench to study them. If he simplified the scrollwork and reduced it so it was only on the flap or even down to a border, it could be done in a lot less time.

He turned around to face her. She had her hands clasped tightly in her lap. "You would have to do the artwork. I have no skill at drawing. We'd have to reduce the size and area of the decorations, but I think you are onto something."

Her smile lit up her entire face. "You do?"

Her joyful expression was more than payment enough for any added work. "Let's finish what we have cut. Tomorrow I'll teach you the basics of tooling leather and we'll see if we can produce a sturdy leather purse that someone will gladly part with their money to own."

"Gabe, please. Speak a little slower."

He swallowed a tinge of annoyance. It wasn't her fault. He would have to learn she couldn't always follow his long, rambling conversations. "Tomorrow I'll teach you to tool. Hopefully someone will want to buy your purses."

"They will. I'm sure of it."

He pointed to the stitcher. "Get on with your work so you can enjoy an afternoon at the picnic."

Her smile vanished as she crossed her arms and raised her chin. "I'm not going unless you go."

"You've just given me more projects to get done, and besides, Lilly is expecting to see you."

"Then she will be disappointed, and it will be your fault. I think if you promise to speak to all my sisters today and to visit with each of them in the evenings, I believe Waneta will be satisfied and continue to let me help you. Provided you make her understand ours is only a working relationship."

That's all it was.

Only could it be more? He liked her. A lot. Spending an hour or so with each of her sisters in the evening would be a waste of time, he already knew that. But if it meant spending the majority of the day with Esther working beside him, it would be worth it.

"Well?" she asked.

"It's a deal."

"Did I hear you right? You'll do it? And you'll come to the picnic?"

"You heard correctly."

"I thought so." Her smile returned.

He grew serious. "There is one problem."

"Oh?"

"I don't want one or more of your sisters to get their hopes up. They could misinterpret my attention."

She frowned. "I hadn't thought of that. You're right. That would never do."

He could get to know the sisters, but he wouldn't raise anyone's hopes. Not even Waneta's. Somehow he had to make his cousin understand that he needed Esther's help.

She turned around and sat at the sewing machine. "I'll get as much work done as I can before my stepmother starts finding other tasks for me."

Since Esther wasn't looking at him, Gabe knew she was finished with their conversation. He knew a moment of envy. She could shut herself off from anyone and any problem simply by not looking. It had to be a small consolation for all that she was missing in the world. He followed her lead and set to work.

Several hours later the door opened and Waneta stepped in. She frowned at Esther, who hadn't seen her yet. Gabe moved quickly to speak with his mother's cousin. "Good morning, Waneta. How are you and your family this morning?"

"We were wondering where Esther had gotten off to. I see she is troubling you again."

"Never think that. She has been a wonderful help. It was nice getting to work with Pamela yesterday, but Esther needs little direction and she is amazingly skilled at leatherwork. She is making my job easier."

He paused, not certain his parents would approve of what he had to say, but he did need Esther's help. "I'm sure my mother has shared her concerns about the family's financial situation. I know how close the two of you are."

Waneta drew back. "She hasn't mentioned anything to me."

"Then perhaps I shouldn't. I don't want to spoil your visit."

"How would our visit be spoiled?"

"I confess Jonah told me you and *Mamm*

had hoped to spark a romance or two between the families."

"Did he? I must speak to the boy about that."

"Don't. None of my brothers are opposed to the idea of finding the right woman, but now may not be the right time."

"How so?"

"Please don't mention this to *Daed* or *Mamm*."

"I can't promise that until I hear what you have to say."

He hoped he was doing the right thing. "Business hasn't been good since we moved here. If things don't improve before the fall, my brothers will have to leave to find work in the city or even return to Pennsylvania. I don't believe they will consider taking wives this year with such an uncertain future."

"Your mother never mentioned this in her letters."

"I'm not surprised. *Daed* did not want to worry her and only shared this news with her recently. As you can imagine, she is concerned about her sons moving away. She has been looking forward to your visit for ages. Having you here is a blessing for her. She has missed you and her friends back home. The thing is, I think I may have a solution to our troubles."

"How so?"

He gestured behind him, where Esther was still sewing. "If I can sell enough of my leather goods, expand this part of the family business, my brothers can remain here working with *Daed* and look to the future with more confidence. Amish families will move here. We'll be the only buggy makers for two hundred miles. We just have to hold on until that happens."

"I see."

"I hope you do. I've rented a booth at our upcoming festival to sell my goods to the *Englisch* tourists who attend. I need a well-stocked inventory of items for people to buy and to place orders for more." He gripped his sore arm. "I'm not going to achieve that without help."

"Can't your brothers work with you?"

"They do when I'm making harnesses. For the smaller items, I need someone who knows how to sew and sew well. None of them have mastered the skill. I can't tell you how grateful I am that Esther offered to help. Without her I don't know what I would do. She's a fine worker. I only wish I could pay her for her labor."

"I'm sure that isn't necessary. We are family after all."

"Still, it doesn't feel right. I'll keep track of her hours and reimburse her when I'm able. With her help I may even have time to get to know your charming family instead of working out here until late at night. I know you must miss Esther's company. If you need her, I will manage somehow."

Waneta raised her fingers to her lips and tapped them. "Now that I understand better, and you're sure she isn't a bother, I'll allow her to continue assisting you. She is handy with a needle."

"You are a dear, Cousin Waneta. I'm glad you and your family are here. It will take *Mamm's* mind off her worries, and perhaps in a few weeks and with the Lord's blessing we'll put an end to her concerns and she can focus on her real goals."

"Which are?"

"Getting grandchildren. She constantly reminds her sons that she isn't getting any younger. And neither are my brothers and I."

"She *should* remind you. Grandchildren will be a great comfort to her in her old age. Esther may continue to help for as long as you want."

Gabe patted his cousin's hand. "*Danki.* I knew you'd understand."

"Your mother sent me to tell you breakfast is ready."

"I'll let Esther know."

"Her deafness makes her such a bother."

Until that second he had been thinking he'd misjudged Waneta. He let go of her hand, struggling to keep his disgust from showing. "It doesn't bother me," he said in a flat tone.

"Your attitude is a credit to your parents and your upbringing."

"All Amish consider children with disabilities a special gift from *Gott* to be treasured by the entire community," he reminded her, since she wasn't practicing her faith where Esther was concerned.

"That is true, but when such a child refuses to be healed, she can only be considered willful and ungrateful."

He glanced at Esther and then back at Waneta. "What do you mean? Are you saying Esther's deafness can be cured?"

# *Chapter Seven*

Gabe waited for Waneta to answer his question. She simply shrugged and walked away, leaving Gabe confused. He looked to where Esther was working. If her hearing could be restored, why wouldn't she do it?

Should he ask her? If Waneta spoke the truth, there had to be a good reason why Esther chose to remain as she was. Perhaps her family couldn't afford the cost, or she didn't wish to burden them with the expense. He had no idea what it would even entail. He recalled her turning down the nurse's offer of information about a hearing aid. He also remembered that Nancy had taken a copy of the brochure from the clinic. Maybe Nancy could explain Waneta's remark.

He walked to Esther's side and touched her shoulder. She looked up at him with a smile. "Is breakfast ready?"

He nodded. She got up from her chair. "*Goot*, I'm starving. We made a lot of progress, didn't we?"

"We did."

"Enough for you to feel comfortable going to the picnic?"

He smiled at her. "As long as we can keep up this pace tomorrow and the next day and the day after that."

"If my stepmother agrees that I may continue working with you."

"She has already agreed. You are free to help me for as long as needed."

"She said that? When?"

"I spoke to her a few minutes ago. She came to tell us breakfast was ready. I explained the situation, and she readily agreed with me." He rubbed his hand over his sore arm. Would Esther be embarrassed or annoyed that they had discussed her behind her back?

Her eyes narrowed suspiciously as she stared at him. "What else did Waneta say?"

Maybe now wasn't the time to reveal Waneta's accusation. There was already too much animosity between Esther and her stepmother. He didn't want to add to it. "Not much. I thought you were hungry?"

Esther relaxed. "I am. Your *mamm* makes the best biscuits. I hope she shares the recipe with Nancy."

"I'm sure she will." He led the way outside. His concerns about Waneta's comment could wait for another time.

After a quick breakfast, Gabe and Esther returned to the shop and managed to get in a few more hours of work before his mother came to the door. "We're ready to go. Are you coming?"

"Esther has convinced me to join you."

"Then Esther has my thanks. But hurry. We don't want to be late when people are coming especially to meet my cousin and her family. We need to stop at the Jefferson farm first. Who knows how long that will take."

He glanced to where Esther was seated with her back to the door. He would have to rearrange the sewing machine and stitcher so that she could have a view of anyone who walked in. That way she wouldn't be excluded from conversations. "I'll tell her that you're ready."

He went back to Esther and tapped her on the top of the head. She tilted her head back and looked at him. "Are they ready?"

"Come along. It was your idea for me to waste an entire afternoon."

She turned around to face him. "I didn't get any of that. It seems I can't speech-read upside down."

He chuckled. "I said time to go." He nodded toward the door.

She sighed heavily. "I guess we should get it over with."

"My thoughts exactly. Do you have your sketchbook?"

She lifted a quilted bag from the floor beside her chair. "Right here."

"Okay." He held out his hand to help her up.

Esther gave Gabe her hand and allowed him to pull her to her feet. The grip of his strong calloused fingers made her heart stumble as her breath quickened. She looked into his bright blue eyes and saw them widen in surprise. They stared at each other for what seemed like an eternity. Did he feel it? This strange connection that seemed to arc between them.

She looked down and pulled her hand away. Such a simple gesture shouldn't affect her and yet it did. She moved past him quickly, determined to gather her wits and pretend nothing had happened. Because nothing had. It was only her imagination. Or maybe a lack of sleep plus her head injury had affected her senses.

She couldn't be attracted to Gabe. They were working partners for the little time she had left in Maine. Nor could she forget that she owed him her life. She wouldn't repay him with unwelcome attention. He wasn't interested in dating any more than she was. They were friends and coworkers. That was all.

Outside she saw both families were seated on hay bales in the back of a large wagon. Two massive black draft horses were hitched to it. Their harnesses gleamed as shiny black as their coats. Chrome tacks and buckles decorated their breast bands and the bridles. Chrome bells jingled as they tossed their heads.

Esther stopped to look up at Gabe. He shrugged. "I know their harnesses are much too fancy for an Amish family. It's called a parade style. We have promised to show a prospective client what the harnesses look like when in use. He has asked my father to stop by his farm today."

"I hope your bishop won't object to such a display at the picnic," her sister Julia said as she helped Esther climb in.

Jonah who was seated on a large wooden box behind the driver's bench seat began to sign. "The bishop won't." **He patted the box he was sitting on.** "We have their regular harnesses with us. If the customer likes the look of the fancy ones he may buy them on the spot. The bishop is the one who gave the man Zeke's name."

**"They're beautiful."**

"According to Gabe this harness style has a three-strap breeching with a scalloped spider. It also has decorated traces and hip drops. The spots are steel and standard size. Gabe could decorate them with diamonds shapes or even stars if the fellow wants that. He put a lot of work into these."

**She smiled at her brother and signed,** "You like Gabe, don't you?"

"He's a fine fellow. He never tells me I ask too many questions. His brothers are nice, too."

**Esther sat back and watched her sisters converse with Gabe's brothers who were seated across from them. She tried to gauge the amount of interest between the couples. Moses and Nancy seemed the**

most at ease with each other. They were frequently laughing about something. Since Nancy wasn't signing, Esther had no idea what they were saying. She didn't have a full view of her mouth.

Julia was seated across from Asher. To Esther's eye they showed little interest in each other. Pamela, on the other hand was showing a great deal of interest in Seth. It was hard to miss. She gazed at him with the eyes of a lovesick puppy. Esther couldn't tell if he was interested in return or not. While he occasionally glanced at Pamela for the most part he kept his eyes riveted to the tips of his boots. Waneta sat up front with Talitha and Zeke but she glanced back frequently.

Gabe leaned forward and gained Julia's attention. Esther couldn't see his face. She looked at Jonah. "What is he saying?" she signed.

"He asked if she was enjoying her visit so far. Please don't make me sign through the entire picnic."

Esther flushed. "I'm sorry. Enjoy the ride and keep an eye out for any moose."

The farm where they stopped was two miles past Lilly Arnett's place. The man who came out of the barn to look over the harness was a short stout fellow with curly black hair. Glancing around, Esther saw eight matching black draft horses inside the corral and several brightly painted antique carriages and wagons parked in a long low shed. Gabe and his father got down to speak to the man. Together they walked around Zeke's horses as the man closely inspected the harnesses.

When Gabe returned to his seat Esther could tell he was disappointed. "He didn't want to purchase them?"

"He wants to think it over. Something tells me we won't hear from him again."

"The harnesses are beautiful."

Gave managed a rueful smile. "*Danki.* I spent many hours making them. Our price is reasonable. I don't know what more he wants. He just purchased a new team of eight horses and was talking about getting parade harnesses for an eight-horse hitch. It would have been a substantial sale for us. Maybe the difference between keeping my brother's home and seeing them leave."

"Someone else will buy them if he doesn't."

"I don't think they are what our Amish neighbors are looking for. It's rare to find a local *Englisch* customer for my harness work. Hank Jefferson and his horses travel to many events around New England. He also gives sleigh rides to the tourists in winter. He would've provided a good way to showcase my work far beyond New Covenant."

"Perhaps he'll change his mind and buy them after all."

"Let's pray that's true."

After changing out the harnesses and stowing the fancy ones in the box behind the wagon seat, the family headed toward the schoolhouse in New Covenant. When they arrived there were already a dozen buggies and carts lined up in front of the building. Food was being laid out by several women on long tables. There were colorful quilts spread under the shade of nearby trees. Adults clustered together in groups while the children played on the school ground equipment.

Esther and her sisters piled out of the wagon and stood off to the side while the Fisher brothers and Jonah unloaded several blue-and-white coolers and carried them to the tables. Talitha and Waneta gestured to the girls to follow them.

Esther kept her chin up and a smile on her face. This would be the hard part. With so many new people to meet and all of them talking she would never know where to look. The result was that people often felt ignored by her if she didn't respond to them. It was easier to remove herself from the group and pretend she wanted to be by herself. If she took her sketchbook and went to sit under a tree who would care?

She saw Gabe smiling at her and knew he would. She suffered through the introductions to a dozen women from the New Covenant church district, including the bishop's wife. Nancy and Julia took turns signing for her. They casually explained that she was deaf but could read lips if people spoke slowly and looked directly at her. The women all started out speaking that way but as more families arrived the conversations became livelier and less directed at her. One by one her sisters moved away as they met other people. Soon there wasn't anyone to sign for her. She lost the gist of the conversation going on around her. Awkwardness kept her looking at her feet more and more.

She glanced up and saw Lilly Arnett getting out of a small blue pickup. She happily left the group she was with and hurried toward her. Lilly smiled, waved and waited until Esther stopped in front of her. "I'm glad you decided to come," Esther said.

"I didn't want to miss a chance to meet your family and introduce you to some of my friends."

A tall teenage boy came jogging over to them. Lilly took Esther by the arm and turned her to face the boy. "This is Harley Gingrich. He works for me when he isn't in school."

Harley nodded to Esther and pointed at the picnic basket Lilly was carrying. "I'll take this to the table."

Lilly handed it over, and Harley walked away. "Harley's brother is Willis. He is our local blacksmith. He recently married the new Amish schoolteacher. Her name is Eva. They are raising Willis's siblings. Harley, Otto and little Maddie, who will be in the second grade when school starts again. Maddie had a most interesting imaginary friend named Bubble who got up to all kinds of mischief. I'm told Bubble moved away to Texas. I think we all miss her."

"Which one is Maddie?" Esther asked using it as an excuse to look for Gabe. He stood with a group of clean-shaven men that Esther knew were bachelors. Only married Amish men wore beards.

Lilly tapped Esther's arm and pointed toward the swings where one little blonde Amish girl was pushing another. "Maddie is on the swing. That is Annabeth Beachy pushing her. Annabeth lives with her mother, Becca, and her grandfather Gideon on a dairy farm not far from here."

Esther was impressed. "You know a lot of the Amish folks in this area."

"I met most of them under unusual circumstances last fall when Maddie followed Bubble into the woods and got lost. Everyone came together to search for her and many of us have remained friends ever since."

"It's amazing how the Lord can use a difficult or frightening time to bring about good things."

"It is. Isn't that how you met Gabe?"

Esther felt a blush warm her cheeks. "It was very frightening."

"Then something good will surely come of it. Did you bring your sketchbook?" Lilly asked.

"I did." Esther opened her bag and pulled

out her drawing pad. Lilly took it from her and began to slowly turn the pages. Finally she looked at Esther. "These are wonderful."

*"Danki."*

"Would you sell some of them to me? I'd love to frame them and hang them on the wall of my breakfast nook."

"You can have them. You don't need to pay me. Choose the ones you want."

"May I keep this and look through it again later."

"Of course."

"Thank you. I see Gemma Crump and Jesse. I need to speak to Jesse about getting a larger garden shed. Excuse me."

Lilly walked away and Esther found herself alone. She moved to the shade of a maple tree and watched the people gathering together near the tables. There were a few *Englisch* but most of the picnic goers were Amish. The women clustered together in small groups. Several of them held babies. The younger children were chasing each other in a game of tag. Several teenagers began setting up a volleyball net. The married men stood near the tables visiting and laughing. She could see people's mouths moving but she couldn't tell what they were saying. Everyone was talking to someone. Everyone but her. A heavy ache centered itself in her chest. It hurt to be ignored, to be overlooked by the people she that had secretly hoped would accept her. She blinked back tears.

Suddenly she was glad she was going home in nine days. She missed her Deaf friends. They understood what it was like to be on the outside looking in. But when they were together it didn't matter. There was joy in signing freely. Among her friends she didn't have to stare at someone's mouth to understand what they were saying.

From the corner of her eye she caught sight of Gabe. He motioned her over. She rose and walked across the grassy lawn to where he stood with a group of young men near his own age. He smiled at her. "These are the fellows I'd like you to meet. I've told them about your hearing. Shall I get Jonah to sign for you?"

It was kind of him to offer. Had he noticed that her sisters had abandoned her? "I think I can manage."

She nodded to each of the men as Gabe introduced them. The one to Gabe's left was Danny Coblentz. "Happy to meet you, Esther. Gabe tells us you have been a great help to him. I'm the new school-teacher. I've taken my sister's place after she married, but she continues to help me find my way with the children."

Gabe turned to his right. "This is Tully Lange. He's a newcomer, not yet Amish but working toward joining us."

Esther had never met an *Englisch* person who wanted to join the Amish faith. Tully tipped his hat and started speaking but Esther couldn't quite understand him. She got "cowboy" and "dairy" but couldn't make sense of what he was saying.

"I'm sorry. I'm afraid I didn't catch that." She looked at Gabe.

"Tully is a cowboy from Oklahoma. He

works with Gideon and Becca Beachy on their dairy farm."

"Does he have an accent?"

Gabe chuckled as he looked at his friend and then back to her. "He has a terrible Western drawl."

"That would explain it." She smiled at Tully. "It may take me longer to learn to understand you because of that. I'm used to our Amish way of speaking."

The third man was Jedidiah Zook. He was a tall lean fellow with a somber expression. He looked toward where her sisters were standing with Waneta.

"Have you met my sisters?" Esther asked.

"Not yet," he said but he looked hopeful.

"Let me introduce you." She pasted a smile on her face and walked toward her stepmother. "Waneta, this is Jedidiah Zook. He is a friend of Gabe's. These are my sisters Julia, Pamela and Nancy."

Waneta's eyebrow rose a fraction. "My stepdaughters and I are happy to make your acquaintance. Are you also a farmer?"

"I have a nice place along the river between here and Fort Craig."

"You must tell us about it," Waneta said with a genuine smile.

Esther turned on her heels and went in search of Lilly. She found her seated on a blanket beside the school leaning back against the building and balancing a paper plate loaded with food on her lap. Esther sat down across from her.

"The Amish ladies in this community sure know how to cook. I never miss a chance to eat with them." Lilly laid her plate aside. "I'll choose a few sketches so you can have your book back."

"You can do that after your lunch. We have all afternoon."

"True." Lilly picked up her plate again. "Your sisters seem to be gathering admirers."

Esther looked over her shoulder. Danny had joined Jedidiah along with another man Esther hadn't met. "Who is the younger fellow with them?"

"That's Ivan Martin. He recently started a small engine repair business."

"He looks young to have his own business already. Most fellows in their late teens are still working with their fathers."

"Ivan is an orphan. He lives with his sisters Jenny and Bethany. Bethany is married to Michael Shetler. He owns a clock and watch repair shop. I see Gabe coming this way."

He sat down next to Lilly so that he was facing Esther. His plate was piled high with ham, corn on the cob, potato salad, green beans and two slices of pecan pie. "Aren't you eating, Esther?"

"Did you leave anything for me?"

He laughed. "There might be some church spread and bread left."

"That sounds *goot*." Esther was fond of the peanut butter and marshmallow cream mixture that was popular among the Amish.

"Gabe, I saw a bird near the river yesterday that I've never seen before. I looked it up on my computer and I think it might be a swallow-tailed kite. Is that possible?"

"Not likely but I guess it is possible. There have been a few sightings in the state. Was it flying when you saw it? Did it have a white head and body with black-tipped pointed wings and a deep forked black tail?"

"That is exactly what it looked like."

Gabe's eyes lit up with excitement. "Where did you see it?"

"You know where the bog lies west of my cornfield?"

"Sure."

"He was flying over the water and then landed in a dead pine."

"I wonder if he is still in the area. Could you show me? When you're done eating and visiting, I mean. Not right this minute."

Lilly grinned. "I'll eat fast."

He looked at Esther with a huge smile

on his face. "Would you like to go birding with me this afternoon instead of hanging out here?"

# Chapter Eight

Gabe watched a bright smile transform Esther's face. It gladdened his heart to know his simple suggestion made her happy. He wanted to keep her smiling. To see her delight every day she was near him.

"May I bring my sketch pad?" she asked.

"Of course."

"Then I should dearly love to accompany you on another walk in the woods."

"You had best go get something to eat first." He pointed toward the tables. She rose and hurried away.

"Esther is a charming young woman," Lilly said.

Gabe continued to watch Esther as she made her selections from the bounty remaining on the serving tables. "She is. I've never known anyone quite like her."

"You've never known anyone who is deaf?" Lilly asked.

He looked at her. "It isn't Esther's deafness that makes her unique. At least not to me." With a jolt he realized he was beginning to like Esther much more than he should. Why did he find her so attractive? He barely knew her.

"Still, it takes a special person to overlook what many would see as a drawback to a relationship where free communication is impossible."

He sighed and looked down at his plate. "It can be difficult. Sometimes I wonder how much of what I say she truly understands and how much she guesses at."

"Have you considered learning sign language?"

He glanced at Lilly again. "Wouldn't that take a long time?"

"I imagine it would take years to become

proficient. Learning a few simple words might not be difficult. I can do some research on the subject if you'd like?"

He saw Esther talking to Jonah. The boy rapidly signed and then took off toward the ballfield where a game was getting underway. Gabe took a bite of ham. He could ask Esther to teach him or he could surprise her by having Jonah show him signs for a few words. He liked the idea of surprising her. "I think her brother might help me with that. Don't say anything to Esther. I might not be able to master a single word."

Lilly chuckled. "I think you'll do much better than that, but I won't tell her."

*"Danki."*

Esther returned and sat down across from him. "Jonah is going to let Waneta know where I've gone so she won't worry. Not that she would."

Gabe let the comment pass. He had no idea how to heal their relationship without knowing the cause of their discord. Maybe one day Esther would confide in him.

It didn't take them long to finish their lunches. Gabe told his father where he was going. His brothers were visiting with friends, except for Moses who was enjoying a game of volleyball while Nancy looked on.

Gabe and Esther got in the pickup with Lilly. "Could you stop by our farm so I can get my binoculars?" he asked.

"Sure. Esther do you need anything?"

Esther didn't answer. She was searching inside her bag. He touched her arm. She looked up with a smile. "What?"

"Lilly wants to know if you need anything from the house."

Esther turned to Lilly. "I need my colored pencils. I thought I had some but apparently I left most of them in my room. Do you mind stopping at the Fisher farm?"

"I don't mind at all," she said making sure Esther was looking at her when she spoke this time.

It didn't take long to reach his farm. Lilly drove faster than Gabe liked, but he didn't say anything to her. He simply wasn't used to speed so he didn't know if hers was excessive. He and Esther quickly gathered what they needed and were soon back in Lilly's truck. She drove to her place and turned into one of her potato fields. Skirting the edge she continued along the bumpy track to a second field, this one planted in corn.

She stopped the truck and pointed. "Follow the edge of this field until you come to a split rail fence. Just beyond it is where the bog starts. Be careful—the ground is mushy. In places you can easily sink up to your knees so stick to the grassy areas. You can spot the dead pine I spoke of from the fence. You know to be careful of the wildlife. The moose have been frequenting this area."

"I'll watch for them." He got out and waited for Esther. She quickly joined him, still grinning. Lilly turned the truck around and drove away.

Esther looked at him. "How does one go about watching for birds?"

"You find a place to get comfortable then watch and listen for their calls."

She chuckled. "I can watch. You'll have to listen."

He smiled. "Come along but watch your step. Stay to the grassy places or you might sink up to your neck in the mud."

"Not how I would want this day to end."

She scrambled over the fence without his assistance. He followed, scanning the area for any sign of moose and saw none. He spotted the dead tree Lilly had mentioned. It was on a small rise of land that jutted out into the bog. It looked like a good place to settle. He should be able to see quite a distance from the base of the tree. He pointed in that direction and Esther nodded. Together they made their way carefully toward the elevated ground. They reached it after about fifteen minutes of circumventing puddles and leaping from one patch of heavy grass to another.

At the base of the tree he noticed a clump of bushes that would provide them with suitable cover. "I think this will do."

"What are we looking for exactly?"

"Birds."

She rolled her eyes at him. "I gathered that much. Any special type of bird?"

"A swallow-tailed kite, but who knows what other interesting species we might discover while we wait to see if he returns to this spot."

"What would tempt him to come back?"

"They feed mostly on flying insects. I understand they like dragonflies and there are plenty of those around. They'll even snatch lizards and snakes out of the trees."

She looked up at the dead branches overhead. "There are snakes in these trees? Why would you want to sit under one?"

He waited until her gaze returned to his. "There aren't any snakes in this tree."

"How can you be so sure?"

"Because I'm familiar with these woods." He hoped he was right. After clearing away some dried pine needles, he sat cross-legged on the ground. He scanned the sky and then raised his binoculars to his eyes.

"Do you see something?"

He lowered his glasses. "Clouds. Aren't you going to sketch flowers?"

"I was until the thought of a snake falling on my head was mentioned."

He chuckled. "I never thought of you as someone who would be scared of snakes."

"They give me the creeps." She scanned the ground around them and looked over the tree again. "Now you know what frightens me. What scares you?"

"Seeing a woman step in front of a speeding truck. That took a few years off my life."

"I am sorry about that. And thank you again for your quick thinking and quick action. What else?"

"Spiders, mice, the usual."

"I don't believe you." She continued to stare at him waiting for his answer.

"I reckon I'm most afraid of failure."

"How so?"

"I'm concerned that my business venture will fail and make things worse for my family instead of better."

"That I can believe. You seem to be a driven person. So what makes you that way?"

"Failures in the past."

"Like what? Business failures?"

He wasn't sure he wanted to dredge up his past mistakes, but Esther was staring at him with such an open and honest expression. Somehow he knew she would understand. "I was engaged to be married once."

"Waneta mentioned it in passing."

"I'm not surprised. She had a lot to say about it back then. The girl was the daughter of her close friend."

"I can imagine she had strong opinions on the subject. What went wrong or do you mind my asking?"

He shook his head. "It was years ago. I fell head over heels for a woman named Gwen, but she secretly wanted someone else. Most Amish couples date quietly and their engagement isn't announced publicly until the banns are read in church. After I proposed and she said yes, Gwen told a lot of people including the fellow she hoped to make jealous. It worked. A month before the banns were to be read she told me it was over between us. She was going to marry the man she truly loved. They were wed on the date she and I had chosen for our ceremony. Did you understand all that?"

It didn't hurt to talk about it as much as he thought it would. Maybe because Esther was such a good listener in spite of being unable to hear.

She nodded. "I got most of it. I understand it must have been a painful time, but why do you consider it your failure?"

"Because I couldn't win her love, nor could I see that she didn't love me. Now I realize it was the best thing for both of us." He had forgiven Gwen long ago but now he could let go of the hurt.

"I was in love once, too," Esther said quietly. "So I understand a little of what you went through."

Gabe saw the pain in her eyes and

reached over to cover her hand with his. "Do you want to talk about it?"

Unexpected tears filled Esther's eyes at his compassion. She looked down at his hand where it rested on hers. He was a good man. "There isn't much to tell. Barnabas King didn't want a deaf wife."

He had seen her as broken, not as a whole person who was simply different. He wanted her to be fixed before he would consider marrying her. This was the life God had chosen for her. She wasn't broken. She wasn't!

Gabe lifted her chin with his fingers so she had to look at him. "Barnabas King sounds like a fool."

She managed a wry smile. "Perhaps I'll think of him that way from now on."

"If I were you, I wouldn't give him a second thought. I know that's easier said than done. But try. You will make some man a fine wife one day."

It would have to be a deaf fellow because no hearing man could understand the way she truly was. She smiled at Gabe's attempt to comfort her. "You aren't getting much bird-watching done."

"And you haven't drawn a single flower." He sat back and raised the binoculars to his eyes.

Esther got out her sketch pad, but it wasn't flowers that interested her. She wanted to draw Gabe. She started with the part of him she liked the best, his mouth. It took her several tries to get it right. It wasn't perfect but she thought she had captured the feeling of his laughter waiting to break free.

What did his voice sound like? She could imagine it a little from the voices she remembered from before she lost her hearing. She recalled her father and her grandfather's voice and the bishop who had preached on Sundays. Gabe's would be different. Softer maybe? Or did he have a gruff growling voice to match his large frame? It was something she would never know.

She rubbed the scar behind her left ear

where a cochlear implant had been surgically placed when she was fifteen. Five years after she lost her hearing. It hadn't been the cure her parents prayed for. Even with therapy and multiple visits to the doctor, the device didn't allow her to hear normally. While she could hear voices and sounds, they were distorted and hard to make sense of no matter how hard she tried. She heard everything through a ringing noise that she finally couldn't cope with. She stopped wearing the external processor after a year and refused to put it back on. She couldn't remove the parts inside her head, but it didn't cause her discomfort. Her father never understood why she wanted to remain deaf. Neither had Barnabas.

She had met him when he came to help repair the special-needs school roof along with a number of young volunteers following a damaging hailstorm. She had been flattered by his interest and had started using her CI again because she wanted to please him. It had been as awful as her first attempts. She only turned it on when they were together. She thought once he learned sign language she would be able to leave it off for good.

He had listed all the reasons why he was a good catch for someone with her problem as if that somehow made up for the fact that he saw her as defective. He couldn't believe it when she turned down his proposal. He had appealed to her father and her new stepmother to pressure Esther into changing her mind. It had driven a wedge between her and Waneta that hadn't yet healed.

Being deaf wasn't always easy, but when she was with other Deaf people it didn't matter. She had a happy and productive life. If she had someone to share her life with, someone who accepted her the way she was, she would be the happiest woman in the world. Her gaze was drawn to Gabe. Someone like him.

Which was a foolish thought. She looked down at her drawing. Gabe was turning out to be a good friend. Something she hadn't expected to find on this trip or ever with a hearing man. She chewed on the end of her pencil for a moment and then drew him smiling with a sparkle in his eyes and tiny crow's feet at their corners. She added the scar to his eyebrow and wondered how he had gotten it.

Gabe lowered his binoculars. She quickly closed her sketch pad. "No sign of the bird you were hoping to see?" she asked.

He shook his head and turned to her. "I saw many species, but not the swallow-tailed kite. I didn't really expect him to remain in this area. Northern Maine is far outside the kite's normal range. Have you found something interesting to draw?"

"Not really."

"Are you wanting to start back?"

"I'm in no hurry. There is enough of a breeze to keep the bugs down and the bog is pretty in its own way." She spied a dark shape moving through a stand of bushes toward them. "Is that my friend the moose again?"

He lifted his glasses briefly and quickly lowered them. He stood up and offered his hand. "We should go."

"Why?"

"Because that is a black bear coming this way."

"What?" She surged to her feet and gripped his arm dropping her sketchbook in the process. "Should we climb a tree or something?"

"It wouldn't do any good. Black bears are excellent climbers. The best thing is to walk, not run, away from them. Bears are more frightened of people than we are of them."

"I doubt that." Her heart hammered in her throat.

Gabe started walking back the way they had come still gripping her hand. She hurried to keep up with him, glancing over her shoulder frequently expecting to see the bear charging toward them. How fast could a bear run?

Gabe glanced at her, squeezed her hand reassuringly but kept walking. If he said anything she couldn't tell. It wasn't until they reached the fence that he stopped and faced her. "He isn't following. I think we're fine."

"Praise the Lord for His mercy."

"Amen."

"That was the first bear I've ever seen. Please don't tell Jonah about this. He'll be out here trying to find him or her in a heartbeat."

"Okay. It will be our secret." He smiled at her, and she realized he was still holding her hand.

His touch was comforting. She managed a smile. "You always seem to be pulling me out of danger. It must be getting old."

"We weren't truly in danger."

"This time." She eased loose from his grip and slipped her hands in the pockets of her apron. "I'm ready to get back to the house."

"Agreed."

She climbed over the fence without his help and together they walked along the edge of the cornfield. When they reached the potato field, he turned into the woods. She thought it was the same path they had been on before but couldn't be sure. Other paths and game trails intersected it. The sun was still high in the sky, pouring in light. The lack of shadows made things look different. When they reached a small pond with the delicate violet growing along the shore she knew where she was. "May I rest a moment?"

He nodded. She sat on a fallen log and tucked a few tentacles of loose hair back under her *kapp*. "I can see how easy it would be to become lost." She smiled at him. "I'm glad you know the way so well."

Gabe sat down beside her. He might know his way around the woods, but he was at a loss for how to handle his growing attraction to Esther. The time he had spent with her had not been boring. "You'll have a lot to tell your friends back home when you write."

"That's the truth."

He wondered what she really thought of

his adopted state. He loved it and wanted her to feel the same. "Have your experiences given you a distaste for Maine?"

"Not at all. I like it here."

"I'm glad. It's a wonderful place to live even when the snow gets five feet deep. You will always be welcome in our home," he said softly.

Would she consider returning to New Covenant someday or even staying on when her stepmother left? She would make a welcome addition to the community. And then he could see more of her.

He gazed into her eyes for a long moment. Did she sense how much he was starting to care about her? Should he tell her? Or was it too soon? They barely knew each other and yet it felt as if he had known her for ages. She put him at ease. He was comfortable with her. Something he couldn't say about any other woman.

Maybe after the festival was over he could explore his feelings more closely and gage her interest in return. When he knew if his endeavor had helped the family or not.

Lilly's suggestion that he learn sign language was a good one. He'd ask Jonah to teach him as soon as they returned home.

Esther looked away first and got to her feet. "I'm ready to go."

He wanted to take her hand again, but she walked on ahead without waiting for him. Maybe she didn't share his growing feelings. Maybe he was reading more into their relationship because he wanted to believe it. The same way he had with Gwen. He did not want to play the fool again.

# Chapter Nine

The following morning Esther hurried down to breakfast with lighthearted steps. She would be spending the day working with Gabe, and she didn't have to worry that her stepmother would be upset. Gabe had seen to that. She was grateful to him for yet another rescue.

She concentrated on her plate of scrambled eggs and sausage in order to keep her eyes off him. It was difficult. Just seeing him smile did funny things to her. She didn't want anyone else to notice how much she liked him. It was her secret.

Julia nudged her with an elbow and

started to sign. "Have you finished our new *kapps*? The day after tomorrow is the church service, and I want to look my best."

"For which brother?" **Esther signed.**

"I didn't say I wanted to impress a Fisher."

"So it is someone you met yesterday."

"Are the *kapps* done or not?"

"I will finish them this morning." It meant she would be late getting out to the workshop, but she had promised to make all of her sisters new head coverings. Since she began working for Gabe, she had put that chore aside.

She looked over and met his gaze. "I will be out to help you directly."

"Is something wrong?" he asked.

"I have some work of my own to finish, that's all."

"Any time you can spare for me is appreciated." He rose with the rest of the men and filed out of the house with them.

Esther helped to clear the table and then raced upstairs to put the ribbons on the *kapps* she had made. It took her nearly an hour. In her haste she made one ribbon longer on the right side of Julia's *kapp.* She had to pick out her stitches and do it over. Satisfied at last, she laid one *kapp* on the end of each cot where her sisters slept. Then she hurried downstairs and out the door. When she reached the workshop, she saw Gabe had turned the sewing table around.

"Do you like it?" He was smiling as if he had done something special.

"It's fine. What was wrong with the way it was facing?"

"You had your back to the door. This way you can see when someone comes in. I can't always be here. I thought this would make it easier for you to see if a customer or someone comes in."

"This is very thoughtful, Gabe. I get better light from the window, too. *Danki.*"

"I'm glad you like it. If there's anything else you want rearranged in here, just let me know."

"This is your shop. You had it set up the

way you like. I'm not going to be here long enough for you to rearrange the equipment on my account."

Some of the happiness left his eyes. "I can always move it back after you're gone."

"Shall we get to work?" she asked.

"Right. I have cut out four of the purses you sketched. Let's see if you can stamp and tool as well as you draw."

Esther pressed a hand to her forehead. "My sketchbook! I left it out at the bog."

"It should be fine. It hasn't rained, and there's none in the forecast. I will fetch it for you tomorrow. I was planning to look for the kite one more time, anyway. You're welcome to join me if you aren't afraid of meeting another bear."

"Or having a snake fall on my head?"

"You'd rather not go. I understand." His disappointment was plain.

She took a quick step toward him. "I didn't say that."

"So you will come?" He looked so hopeful that she didn't have the heart to refuse him—nor did she want to.

"I will be better prepared this time. I'll take my umbrella."

He threw back his head and laughed. She wished she could hear what that sounded like. There were so many things she wanted to discover about him.

The day went by quickly. Esther discovered stamping leather required a strong wrist and accuracy. She couldn't count the number of times she accidentally thumped her thumb and forefinger with a mallet while trying to hit the head of the small tool she held positioned just so on a strip of leather. Gabe made it look easy.

Gabe tried to make everything easy for her. He always made sure he was looking at her when he spoke. He left his own work frequently to check on how she was doing. He made sure she took breaks when she could have spent hours at her machine without stopping. He was almost the perfect boss. She would miss him dearly when she went home.

The following day she left the tooling to Gabe and began stitching the assortment of items he had ready for her. She was pleased with the way her first purse turned out. All it needed was to have a cloth lining added with several pockets to hold keys or cell phones. She would have to ask Lilly what size pockets would be needed, since Esther wasn't sure how big a cell phone was. She had seen them in use and her sister Nancy even had one for a while, but Nancy had given up using it because she intended to be baptized into the faith and cell phones were not allowed by their church district.

Esther held the purse up for Gabe to see. "What do you think?"

He took it from her and examined it inside and out. "Nice work."

"But will it sell?"

"Perhaps we should ask a few of our *Englisch* neighbors what they think?"

"That's a good idea. We can ask Lilly."

He gestured toward the cutting table.

"I've finished here for today. How about you?"

It was early afternoon. She could have kept working. Instead she stretched her tired shoulders. "I'm ready for some fresh air and a little exercise."

He walked to the door and held it open for her. "Let's go over to the bog. I'll get my binoculars. Why don't you wait here?"

She couldn't keep a happy grin off her face as she watched him cross to the house. A walk in the woods with Gabe promised to be the highlight of her day. More wildflowers and his company. What could be better? She saw Jonah coming her way.

He tipped his head to the side. "What are you smiling about?" he signed.

She wiped the grin off her face. "Nothing. Gabe and I are going to do some bird-watching. If anyone wants us, we'll be at the Arnett farm."

"Since when do you like bird-watching?"

"Gabe looks for birds. I look for flowers to collect and draw."

"I still haven't seen a moose. Are you sure he was at the pond by the highway?"

She nodded. "I saw him there twice. Be careful when you are out walking. There are bears about."

His eyes brightened. "Really?"

She scowled at him. "Do you know what to do if you see a bear coming your way?"

"Run?"

"Wrong answer," she said. "Ask Gabe. He will tell you the best way to avoid them."

"I will." Jonah turned and jogged to the house.

Esther smiled as she watched him. Having Jonah to talk with was almost as good as being with her friends. She waited impatiently for Gabe to return.

Gabe had his binoculars and his book on bird identification in his hand when Jonah came rushing into the kitchen.

"Esther says I'm supposed to ask you what to do if I see a bear."

"I thought she wasn't going to tell you that we saw one."

"You did? Where? Esther never said she actually laid eyes on a live one."

"It was a long way from here, and I wasn't supposed to tell you because she's afraid you'll go looking for it."

"I promise I won't."

Gabe nodded and told the boy what he needed to know if he encountered a black bear. He started to leave but stopped and turned to the boy. "Jonah, is it difficult to learn sign language?"

"Not really."

"How could I go about learning to sign? Could you teach me?"

"Sure. If you tell me where you saw the black bear."

Gabe crossed his arms over his chest. "Nope. So thanks, anyway."

"I was just kidding. I'll be happy to teach you some words in sign. Why don't you ask Esther? I'm sure she'd do it."

"I wanted to surprise her."

Jonah folded his arms and cupped his

chin with one hand. "You're sweet on my sister, aren't you?"

"We are friends, but would you have a problem with it if I was?"

"Only that it would make Waneta think she is right about her gift for matchmaking."

"Esther doesn't get along with Waneta. Why is that?"

"They just don't see eye to eye about a lot of things. I'm not sure they ever will. Esther and Waneta can both be stubborn."

Gabe's mother came into the kitchen. "What are you two discussing so intently?"

Jonah winked at Gabe. "Bears." The boy went back outside.

"I like that kid," Gabe said.

"Are you enjoying our visitors? I want our two families to be close friends."

Gabe wagged a finger at her. "You want your sons to fall head over heels for Waneta's girls."

She grinned. "Maybe I do. They are wonderful women. I wouldn't mind having one or more of them as daughters-in-law. What's wrong with that?"

"Nothing, I reckon." They were nice women, but they sometimes neglected Esther. He wasn't sure how to broach the subject but decided he needed to say something. "I did notice that they deserted Esther yesterday at the picnic."

His mother nodded. "I saw that, too."

"Tomorrow is our church service. There will be a lot of visiting afterward. Could you suggest to them that they include Esther rather than leaving her on her own? Without someone to sign for her, she is uncomfortable in a crowd of people."

"I'm not sure it's my place, but I will speak to Waneta. Sometimes we take our family members for granted without realizing that they may need our attention as much as others do."

"I appreciate that, *Mamm*."

"Where are you off to?"

"Esther and I are going over to the Arnett farm to do some bird-watching."

"The two of you have been spending a

lot of time together. Is it because you feel responsible for her after saving her life, or do you feel sorry for her?"

"Neither. The fact that she is deaf makes things more difficult, but I don't pity her. I enjoy her company. She has a very lively mind."

"Her type of deafness is inherited. Any children she might have may also be deaf."

He frowned. "Any of us can have a child born with a disability. *Gott* decides."

"He does, but I thought you should be aware of the fact."

"I'm not planning to marry her, *Mamm*. We've only known each other a few days."

"I knew I was going to marry your father the day I first laid eyes on him. Love comes slowly to some and quickly to others."

Gabe gazed at her intently. "How did you know?"

She clasped her hands over her chest. "My heart lifted when he smiled at me. It may sound silly, but that's how I knew. I couldn't imagine going through life without seeing his smile every day."

"I reckon the Lord didn't want it any other way. For which I am grateful. We'll be back before supper."

"All right. I will speak to Waneta about making sure the girls don't abandon Esther at church."

*"Danki."*

He headed outside and saw Esther waiting for him beside the shop. She came over to join him. As they rounded the barn, Gabe saw Pamela and Seth walking toward them holding hands. They were intent on each other and didn't notice they weren't alone until they were only a few feet away. Seth stopped abruptly and let go of her hand. "Were you looking for me?"

*"Nee,* we are going to do some birdwatching."

"Okay. Have a good time," Seth said as he stepped aside. Gabe walked on, but he heard Pamela giggle behind him. He glanced back. She pressed a hand to her lips and turned away.

"I may not have given Waneta enough credit as a matchmaker," Esther said. She looked over her shoulder. "They seem to have hit it off."

"As have we," Gabe said. She wasn't looking at him, so he knew she couldn't hear him. It was just as well. He had no idea how she felt about him other than a shared friendship. He didn't want to risk losing that by making her uncomfortable.

They traveled through the woods without talking. Twice Esther paused to pluck a few flowers and place them in her pocket. When they reached the pond, Gabe stopped and turned to her. He pointed to the violets she had sketched on their first walk. "Do you want to take some of these?"

She shook her head. "Lilly said they are a rare flower, so I will leave them be. I have my drawings and that is enough."

"What are you going to do with the ones in your pocket?"

"I'll press them and add them to my albums."

"Do you have a lot?"

"Several albums with about thirty flowers in each."

"That's a lot of petals."

She smiled. "The Lord has made a lot of flowers. I'll never gather them all. Just like He has made many types of birds."

He held out his identification book. "I mark off each one that I've seen. Someday I'd like to travel down south to view the egrets and storks of the Everglades."

A small frown appeared on her face. "I'm sorry, I didn't understand that."

He wasn't sure how to say it so she could. How many times had she simply smiled instead of comprehending his words? He tried to phrase it more simply. "I want to visit Florida."

"The Amish community in Pinecrest?"

It was close enough. "That's right. We should get going."

He kept a wary watch for wildlife, but their trip through the bog was uneventful.

She retrieved her sketch pad and brushed off the dirt before sitting down as far away from the tree as she could get without stepping into the bog. He tried not to smile. She saw him struggling.

"Laugh if you want, but I am not going to sit where a snake could fall on me."

"You know there are more of them in the water than in the trees."

She quickly moved back. "Now you tell me. Will we be here long?"

He shook his head then lifted his binoculars to scan the sky and trees. After several minutes he noticed an olive-sided flycatcher perched in a dead tree a few dozen yards away. He glanced at Esther. She was drawing the red-stemmed feather moss.

He touched her shoulder. "Do you want to see a rare bird?"

"Is it the one you had hoped to see?"

"No, but this one is almost as interesting. An olive-sided flycatcher." He pointed to the tree. "He's perched at the very top on that dead limb. He's a gray fellow with a white strip down his chest."

Gabe handed her the glasses. He moved closer to help her focus them. They were sitting shoulder to shoulder. He could easily put his arm around her. Would she object?

"I don't see him. Oh, wait. Now I do. He looks like he's wearing a gray vest over a white shirt. How cute."

She lowered the glasses and turned to Gabe. Her smile faded as she gazed at him. She reached out and touched his lips with one finger. "You have a beautiful mouth."

He sucked in a quick breath. More than anything he wanted to kiss her, but he held himself in check.

She blushed and looked away. "I shouldn't have said that."

He cupped her chin to turn her face toward his. "I don't mind that you like my mouth. I like a lot of things about you."

"Such as?"

"You have amazing expressive eyes.

They look like amber honey in the sunlight. I've never seen anyone with that color."

"I have my mother's eyes."

"I imagine she was a special person."

Esther turned to look out over the water. Memories of her mother were bittersweet. Her childhood had been wonderful, but all that changed. "When I lost my hearing, she couldn't accept it. She took me to doctor after doctor hoping to find a cure. There wasn't one, but she never gave up hope. It consumed her. She neglected my father and my sisters, and they resented it. Eventually our bishop came to speak with her. I don't think she realized the harm she was doing our family until then.

"After that she saw to it that my sisters and I learned sign language, but she didn't stop searching for something that would help me hear again."

She looked at Gabe. He was watching her intently, his eyes full of compassion. "It was *Gott's* will."

"I knew this is the life He has chosen for me. I was content. My mother couldn't understand that. When I was fifteen, she finally found the 'cure' she had been seeking." Esther knew her bitterness was seeping out in her words.

Gabe tipped his head slightly. "Waneta suggested that you refused to be healed. What did she mean?"

Esther picked up a small stick and threw it in the murky water. "She would say that. My father believes the same thing. My parents insisted I have a cochlear implant. A CI is a device that is placed under the skin behind the ear. It bypasses the ear and sends signals to the nerves that carry sounds to the brain. The doctor said the success rate of the operation was nearly one hundred percent."

She hadn't wanted them to spend their life savings on the surgery or to have the entire church pay for her hospital stay, but no one listened to her.

"Is it the same device Nurse Heather talked about?"

"*Nee*, it isn't." She sat staring at the swamp grasses blowing in the breeze for a long time. Finally she looked at Gabe. He was waiting patiently for her to continue.

She sighed. "I had the surgery, but when they turned the device on, it didn't work the way they said it would. I could hear again, but everything was distorted. There was an awful ringing that wouldn't stop unless I turned the implant off. No one believed me when I said it didn't work right. *Mamm* insisted I just needed to get used to it. My parents had sacrificed so much to get the treatment for me that I kept trying. It was awful. Then my mother got sick and died quite suddenly. After that I put my CI away and didn't use it again until I met Barnabas King. After he and I parted ways, I left it off for good. I'm Deaf. I accept it."

"Waneta believes you could hear if you wanted to."

"She thinks I like the attention of being the only deaf person in the family."

"I heard it was an inherited disease. No one else in the family is affected?"

"Both my father and my mother have cousins that are deaf. There is a higher-than-average number of deaf children in our community. That's why a special school was started. I'm a teacher's assistant there, and I love it. I have Deaf friends. We have great times together. Everyone at the school uses ASL. I never have to guess what someone is saying." It was the one place she felt safe and valued for who she was.

"Thank you for telling me this."

She shook her head, amazed and a bit embarrassed by how much she had revealed about herself. "I don't know why I did."

"Maybe because I'm your friend, too."

"I reckon you're right." What would he think if she said she wanted to be more than a friend?

Did she?

Gabe wasn't deaf. He couldn't know what it was like, but he was kind and understanding. Could she overlook the fact that he was a hearing person and grow to care for him? She already liked him more than she thought possible, but would he want to court a deaf woman? How could she risk her heart only to hear she wasn't seen as a whole person by the man who wanted to marry her?

## *Chapter Ten*

Unlike the previous two days, Esther went down to breakfast devoid of any eagerness to greet the day. It was Sunday. The families would be going to the prayer meeting that was held every other week. She was expected to join them.

In her Amish community, there was a bishop and two ministers who shared the preaching during the three-or four-hour service. It was unlikely that she would understand much of what was said today. Preachers normally moved about as they spoke to the congregation or read from the Bible. There would be singing that she couldn't join. Afterward families would visit with each other while the children played together. Her one new friend, Lilly, would not be there this time. While she had met many of the women in the community already, she never felt comfortable in large groups. Today was likely to be a repeat of the picnic, where she watched others enjoying themselves from afar.

The Fisher men were still out doing the morning chores when Esther entered the kitchen. Waneta, Julia, Pamela and Nancy were standing in a semicircle around Talitha. The discussion looked serious, but as soon as Talitha caught sight of her, she smiled and said, "Good morning, Esther. I hope you slept well. How is your headache?"

"Gone. *Danki.*"

Waneta looked right at Esther. "I'm pleased to hear it," she said slowly. She then turned and began cracking eggs into a skillet on the stove.

Esther's sisters all signed, "Good morning." Then they began to pack several coolers with food that would be served for the noon meal.

It was a strange start to the morning but a welcome change. Esther couldn't help wondering what they had been discussing. "What can I do?" she asked.

Talitha gestured toward several boxes sitting at the end of the counter. "If you would take the pies out to the buggy, that would be a help. We're almost ready to go as soon as everyone has had their breakfast."

Esther stacked the two boxes together and went out the door. She met Zeke coming in. He stepped back to let her pass. Gabe was behind him. He took the boxes from her. "Where do you want these?"

"Your mother said in the back of the buggy."

"Can you get the buggy door for me?"

"Of course." She hurried to open it.

After he had the boxes stowed, he leaned against the door frame. "I hope you enjoy the preaching today. Bishop Schultz can be a little long-winded, but he does a fine job."

"You will have to tell me what he preached about afterward. I doubt I'll be able to grasp much of it."

Gabe frowned. "Why?"

"I have yet to meet a preacher who stands still and looks straight at one person for the entire sermon."

"You have a point. He does like to use the room."

"I hope you won't desert me after the meal. That way I know I'll have at least one person to visit with."

"You can count on me, but you will find you are welcome in New Covenant. Others will seek you out to get to know you better. We should go in to breakfast."

She nodded and walked into the house. Everyone was seated at the places. She took her chair across from Gabe and bowed her head for the silent blessing that Zeke would lead. She glanced occasionally at him, waiting for him to signal the end of the prayers. When he did, his sons began passing the plates of food around.

She buttered some toast and sipped her

coffee. She wasn't hungry. She was dreading the morning. At least she might be able to spend time with Gabe in the afternoon.

Everyone finished eating quickly, and the table was cleared. Gabe's brothers carried out the coolers while the women put on clean, crisp white aprons, black shawls and their black traveling bonnets before heading out to the buggy.

She was seated beside the door in the back seat as they got underway. At the end of the lane, they turned out onto the highway. As they passed the large pond where Gabe had saved her life, she saw a moose step out of the forest and into the water. It was a female with twin calves by her side. Esther reached over and tapped Jonah. "There is your moose."

He launched himself across her lap to look out the window. He stared at the animals until the buggy rounded a curve in the road. He looked at her with a huge grin on his face. "A cow with two babies. That was so amazing."

"Better than playing a game of baseball with your friends?" she asked.

"Almost as good as winning against the Mount Hope team."

As his team had only beaten their rival school once, she was glad she'd seen the animals and pointed them out to him.

The church service was being held at the home of members who lived five miles away, on the other side of New Covenant. It took almost an hour to reach the farm. A cluster of buggies was lined up on the side of the hill below the house. Zeke turned into the last row. A boy in his teens came to take the horse. He led Topper away, still in his harness, and tied him up at the corral fence beside the barn, where another dozen or so buggy horses were munching on the hay that had been spread on the ground for them.

An enclosed gray wagon was parked beside the house. A group of men was unloading and carrying in the backless benches that would be used to seat the congregation. Zeke and his sons headed toward the barn where a large group of men stood talking. She recognized Tully, Danny and the bishop among them.

Crops and the weather were no doubt the main topics being discussed. It was that way in every Amish farming community. Zeke took the bishop by the elbow and led him a few feet away from the group, where Gabe joined them. They were soon deep in conversation.

Nancy touched Esther's arm. "How are you and Gabe getting along?" she signed.

"We have a good working relationship. I think we're becoming friends. How are you and Moses doing?"

"He's a very sweet boy. Much more mature than the fellows back home. He plans on being baptized in the fall."

"That sounds promising. Do you like him?"

"I do, but don't tell Waneta. We'll never hear the end of her bragging about her matchmaking skills if she were to suspect Moses and I will be courting."

"He has asked you to walk out with him?" Esther was surprised.

"He knows I am going home at the end of the month. He has asked if he may write to me, and he has invited me to visit again next summer."

"I'm happy for you. The Fishers are a warm and caring family." She would miss Nancy if she moved to Maine, but she wanted her little sister to be happy. It was easy to imagine being content in the Fishers' home.

"I see they are finished unloading the bench wagon. We can go in."

Esther followed her sister inside. Julia and Pamela were already seated. The benches had been set out in rows in the living room with an aisle down the middle. Men would sit on one side of the aisle. The women would sit on the other. Married men and women occupied the front rows, while the single women and men sat behind them. Esther soon realized she and her sisters were almost the only single women in the congregation. There were several young girls but none old enough to be courting. It was no wonder Talitha had hatched a plan with Waneta to bring her stepdaughters for a visit.

Across the way Esther saw the Fisher brothers file in and take their seats. Jonah sat with them. Gabe smiled and nodded to her. Behind him, Danny and Jedidiah were also smiling in her direction. Esther quickly realized their eyes were on Julia and Pamela. Did the Fisher brothers know they were in for some competition?

A few minutes later, the bishop and the ministers came into the room. Nancy turned to Esther. As soon as the bishop began to speak, Nancy began to sign his words. Esther normally sat through a service trying to grasp fragments of what was being said by reading the speaker's lips.

According to Nancy the bishop was informing the congregation that Waneta and her stepdaughters were visiting in the area and that one of the daughters was deaf. Because of that her family members would use sign language to convey the preaching to her.

To Esther's surprise, he held his hand out flat with his palm up and then brought it toward his chest. "This is the sign for 'welcome.' I ask that we all use it to make our deaf visitor feel we are pleased she is among us."

Nearly everyone turned and looked in Esther's direction and repeated the sign. She felt heat rising in her face as she made the sign for "thank you."

Around her people reached for their hymnal, the *Ausbund*, and opened it. She could see the first song had started. Nancy signed the page number, and Esther flipped to the song so that she could read the lyrics even though she chose not to sing. She remembered many hymns from her childhood, but she couldn't be certain she was in tune or in time with others. For the rest of the service, Nancy and Pamela traded off signing for Esther so that she was able to understand all that the bishop and the ministers had to say. The sisters received many curious glances. A toddler in the row ahead of them mimicked the signs as she grinned at Esther.

When the prayer meeting was over, they filed outside so that the benches could be rearranged into tables and seating for the meal. Her sisters stayed close beside her and continued to sign for her as she was introduced again to the members of the community. She became reacquainted with the bishop's wife and the wives of the ministers and their families. Some of the younger women held babies or had toddlers clinging to their skirts. The little girl who had been trying to sign toddled over to Esther and reached up to be held.

Esther picked her up and was struck with a sharp pang of longing to have a family of her own. But that would require a husband. There wasn't one in her immediate future. The child quickly wanted down and went to play with a little boy near her age.

When Esther had a free moment, she

caught Nancy's arm. "I can't tell you how much I appreciate you doing this."

Nancy blushed. "I confess it was Talitha's suggestion."

"You're always so quick to want to do things on your own," Julia signed.

Pamela nodded. "You can be abrupt and self-absorbed. Sometimes we forget that you do need us."

"Of course I need you. You're my sisters." Esther hugged each of them in turn. "I will try not to be abrupt in the future."

"And we'll remind you when you are doing exactly that again." Julia grinned.

Esther gave her another quick hug. "And I'll point out when you're ignoring me."

"I fear we may have some sisterly squabbles in the future," Nancy signed.

"We may, but we'll always make up, because we love each other." Esther wiped a tear from her eye. "Which one of you taught the bishop how to sign 'welcome'?"

Nancy shook her head. "It wasn't us."

Then it must have been Jonah. "I need

to thank Talitha for her thoughtful suggestion."

She found Waneta and Gabe's mother in the kitchen setting out the food with some of the other women. "Talitha, my sisters tell me I have you to thank for encouraging them to assist me today."

"It wasn't my idea. I merely pointed out to some members of your family that they were being unkind, although I know that was never their intention." She looked at Waneta.

"Of course it wasn't the girls' intention," Waneta said.

"Did Jonah tell you I dislike crowds?"

"Actually, it was Gabe who mentioned it. He taught the bishop the sign for 'welcome.' That was his idea, too," Talitha said with a knowing smile.

"Gabe did?" For her.

"He thinks a great deal of you," Waneta said.

Esther kept her face carefully blank. "I value him as a friend, too. Excuse me. I need to thank him."

Outside she caught a glimpse of Gabe watching from across the way. He was leaning against an empty hay wagon. She crossed the distance between them with her heart pounding in her chest. How could she adequately thank him for everything he had done?

She stopped in front of him and placed her hands on her hips. "I understand you taught the bishop the sign for 'welcome.' Who taught you?"

He spelled out "Jonah" in sign.

Her jaw dropped. "Why did you do this?"

"Because I didn't like the way your sisters ignored you."

"We used to be close. Now I hope we can be that way again. We simply got used to going our separate ways."

"I'm glad if I helped."

She found herself swamped with emotions. Gratitude and something else. A sincere warmth for this man filled her heart. If she wasn't careful, she would blurt out how special he made her feel. "I have a sign name. Deaf people often choose one so they don't have to spell it out each time. Would you like to know it?"

"Sure."

"It's the sign for 'flower.'" She made the motion of holding a flower by the stem and bringing it to her nose to sniff.

"Flower. It suits you." He repeated the sign.

"I should get back to my sisters."

"That's fine. Enjoy the day. We have plenty of work waiting for us tomorrow."

She took a step back. "It's the kind of work I don't mind if you're there to help." She clamped her lips shut and spun on her heels. She managed to walk, not run, away from him and her growing feelings for this generous and thoughtful man.

Gabe smiled as she walked off. He was glad he had managed to improve her relationship with her sisters and allow her to understand the preaching today. Hearing the words God moved their ministers and bishop to speak brought them all closer to

God and to each other. No one should be alone in this life.

Seth stopped beside Gabe. "You like her a lot, don't you?"

He couldn't fool his brother, so he didn't try. "I do."

"I think she likes you, too."

"As a friend."

"Maybe a little more than that?" Seth suggested.

"She doesn't want a hearing fellow. She has made that plain."

"Maybe that is what her head says. Sometimes the heart leads one down an unexpected path."

"Is that what happened to you? Pamela and you seem fond of each other in spite of the fact that you claimed you had no interest in finding a wife yet."

"I'm not ready to marry her, but I do like her a lot. Should I ask her to be your go-between and find out if Esther is interested in dating you?"

Gabe considered it. The question would be better coming from someone who knew how to talk to Esther. But was the time right?

He decided against the idea. "*Danki*, but not yet."

He needed Esther to help him finish his work before the festival. If she found out he was interested in courting her and she didn't return those feelings, she might be uncomfortable working with him. It was more than her sewing skills he wanted to keep. Seeing her every day all day long made him happy. He couldn't risk losing that.

What he wanted to say could wait until after the festival. By then perhaps his lessons with Jonah would give him a good enough grasp of sign language to make himself understood without worrying that she didn't get what he was trying to say.

Later in the afternoon, when the families had returned from the church service, Gabe was reading a book in the living room when Esther and Jonah came in. Jonah sat on the sofa beside Gabe while Esther sank to the floor in front of him.

He closed his book, keeping his finger between the pages to hold his place. "Did you want something?"

Eagerness filled her amber-colored eyes and made them sparkle. "Bethany Shetler mentioned there is a farmers market in Fort Craig every Wednesday afternoon during the summer."

"That's true. Do you have produce you wish to sell? Have you been growing radishes on the side?" He could see that Jonah was signing everything he said.

Esther rolled her eyes. "Be serious a moment. Bethany told me her husband takes some of his clocks to sell, so it doesn't have to be just vegetables. Apparently a lot of *Englisch* people come to it."

"I've seen a fair number of them there. What is your point?"

"That the farmers market might be a good place to see how well your items sell, particularly the purses we have made."

He rubbed his chin as he considered the idea. "There is some merit in your suggestion. But none of the purses are lined yet. How many could we have finished by Wednesday? We still have a lot of pieces to make before the festival."

"I've talked to my sisters, and they are all willing to sew linings for us. We could have a dozen done to take, plus a few of your other items to show people samples of what you make. I said you couldn't depend on a single festival for your income. Selling at this market could give you income all summer long after the festival is finished. What do you think?"

"I think it is something we should try to see if it is indeed worth our while."

She clapped her hands together. "I knew you would see the benefits. Perhaps your mother has some leftover fabric from her quilting we can use without adding the expense of buying new material. I'll go ask her."

Gabe leaned forward and put his hand on her head to stop her from rising. "It is Sunday. A day of rest. We do only essential work on the Lord's day."

"Asking about supplies and looking to see what's available isn't working."

He tipped his head. "Isn't it?"

She nodded. "Okay. Maybe I am getting carried away."

He removed his hand and sat back. She sighed deeply. "What are you reading?"

"A book about birds."

"Is there something you don't already know in it?"

"The author talks about how the migration patterns of birds are changing due to the changes in our climate."

"Must be fascinating." Her expression said just the opposite.

He held back a smile. "Shall I read some since Jonah is here to interpret?"

Jonah shook his head and stood up. "I'm going to play a game or two of horseshoes with Moses."

The boy left the room, leaving Esther still sitting at Gabe's feet. He closed his book and put it aside. "What do you like to read?"

She crossed her arms and raised her

nose in the air. "What makes you think I enjoy reading?"

"You have a sharp mind. I can't imagine you would ignore all books have to offer."

She chuckled. "I do like to read. I enjoy mystery stories and some romances."

"Love stories? You seem so practical. I wouldn't have pegged you as a romantic."

"Well, I am. I think there is someone out there for everyone. Despite the obstacles that life places in our way, the Lord will see that faith and love win the day."

He leaned forward to gaze into her eyes. "Do you truly believe that?"

# Chapter Eleven

Esther gazed up at Gabe. His bright blue eyes were fixed on her intently. What was he thinking? She knew in her heart that this was about more than his question. She did believe there was someone for everyone. Gabe would certainly make some woman a wonderful husband. Esther cared for him dearly, but they weren't meant for each other. Had she given him the impression that she thought they might be? Was that what he wanted to know?

She wouldn't hurt him for the world. She had to convince him that his friendship was all that mattered. Because it did, more than she could say.

"I fervently pray the Lord has someone in mind for me to love. A man I can respect and who respects me in return. One who understands what it is to be deaf in a hearing world. I pray *Gott* has a kind and generous woman in mind for you to love, too."

Gabe sat back. His gaze became shuttered. "We have both been disappointed in the past. I admire that you still believe in love."

"Don't you?"

"I hope to marry someday. I want a family. But trusting that a woman has my best interest at heart is hard."

"I know what you mean. It is difficult, but at least we know what we want."

Hearing Barnabas tell her that she needed to be "fixed" before he could marry her had crushed her. It had taken a long time and the wise counsel of her Deaf friends for her to recover her self-esteem. She never wanted to feel that despondent again.

She rose. "I will let you get back to your reading."

"What will you do this evening?"

"I may take my sketch pad outside. Your mother has a lovely flower garden."

"Would you like to take a walk? We can choose a different path through the woods. Perhaps you can discover some new wildflowers."

"I would like that."

He got to his feet and nodded toward the window. "Our challenge may be avoiding other couples strolling in the woods."

She looked out and saw Danny talking to her sister Julia in the garden. They headed toward the gate that led to a grove of fruit trees behind the house.

"I'm glad I straightened the ribbons on her *kapp*."

Gabe gave her an odd look. "What does that mean?"

"She was insistent that I finish a new head covering for her before church today. This explains whom she was hoping to impress. Let me get my sketch pad."

She hurried upstairs, eager to spend more time with Gabe. He wasn't the man for her. She accepted that, but she still cherished their time together. What little of it they had left.

When she returned, he was waiting with his binoculars and his birding book. Together they went out the back door and across the garden. At the gate he took a path that led away from the orchard. They crossed a small meadow with a lone gnarled tree at its center. The remnants of an old rock wall extended a few feet out from its trunk. He took a seat and raised his binoculars to his eyes. Esther settled herself on the ground. A cluster of small yellow flowers were poking their heads out from between the blades of grass. She opened her sketchbook and was soon trying to capture their beauty silhouetted against the moss-covered rocks behind them.

When she finally looked up, she saw Gabe had set his binoculars aside and was watching her. "No birds?" she asked.

"Ordinary ones. Nothing special in the skies or the trees this evening. What did you find?"

She handed him her pad. "I don't know the name, but they are very pretty and delicate."

"They're called Quaker ladies."

"Are there flowers called Amish ladies anywhere?"

"I see a lovely one right in front of me."

She felt a blush rising to her face. "I'm sure I don't compare favorably to these beauties."

"I'm forced to disagree." He looked through the pages at the drawings she had made. He paused at one page and then closed the pad.

"Are you ready to go back?" she asked.

"*Nee*, I'm content right here." He handed her sketchbook back to her. "Don't let me interrupt you."

She tried to concentrate on drawing a small blue violet she spied a few feet away, but she couldn't keep her mind on what she was doing with Gabe staring at her.

She looked at him. "It's disconcerting."

"What is?"

"You. Gawking at me."

"I was studying your mouth."

She raised her fingers to her lips. "Why?"

"You once told me I had a pretty mouth."

"I shouldn't have said that."

"You captured a good likeness of someone's lips." He nodded toward her drawing pad.

She had forgotten this one contained the sketches she had made of him at the bog that day. "I spend a lot of time looking at people's mouths."

"I was trying to imagine what that must be like."

"Would you kindly stop staring at mine?"

"It's pleasing. I like the way you smile. It sneaks out like you aren't quite ready for it, but then you give in and it's lovely."

She stared at her hands. "Now you're making fun of me."

He reached out to lift her chin until she was looking at him. "Not in the least."

She noticed something beyond him in the sky. "You are missing what you came here for."

"I came here to spend an hour with you."

"I thought you came out here hoping to see the swallow-tailed kite. He's flying over your left shoulder."

"Is he?"

She cocked one eyebrow. "Aren't you going to look?"

"I've discovered observing flowers is more interesting than watching birds."

Esther wasn't sure she understood him, but there was no mistaking the tenderness in his eyes. He was making it almost impossible to pretend that friendship was all she wanted.

Gabe realized his mistake almost as soon as the words were out of his mouth. His intention had been to keep their relationship friendly. It wasn't to reveal his growing attraction to her. But gazing at her lovely face so close to his own was almost his undoing. He had to put some distance between them.

"It's getting late. We should head back." He got to his feet and clenched his hands into fists so he wouldn't reach out to help her up. He didn't trust himself to hold her hand and not pull her into his embrace. He moved a few steps away.

"Okay." She scrambled to her feet and dusted off her skirt. She gathered her drawing materials and put them in her bag.

He started walking. After a few steps, he glanced back to make sure that she was following. She kept her eyes downcast. Maybe she didn't want to know if he spoke again. He told himself it was for the best. She was praying that God would bring a deaf man for her to love. Someone who understood her silent world.

Gabe gave a heavy sigh. She would never believe that he could be such a man.

"Are you in a hurry?"

He stopped and looked back. He had

outpaced her by several yards. "I'm sorry. I was lost in thought."

"Then I'm sorry I interrupted."

He waited for her to catch up. "Don't be. I was being rude."

"Were you thinking about the farmers market?"

Not until she mentioned it, but it was a safe subject. "I may purchase some dyed leather from my supplier. The dog collars and purses might do better if they were more colorful. What do you think?"

"I like the idea. Will you be able to get it soon enough? We absolutely need pink."

"Maybe not a large assortment of colors. It wouldn't be wise to invest heavily in something until we know if it will be popular. I'm supposed to have my stitches out tomorrow. I'll stop at Ed Carson's when I'm done at the clinic and see what he has available. He tans hides. I know he has some leather already dyed. I can order more if your plan works."

"If? Do I detect some doubt?" A spark of defiance appeared in her eyes. "May I remind you that you doubted my ability to sew leather goods."

He decided to goad her a little. "I may have been wrong once, but developing a marketing plan isn't like planning a meal for the family."

She crossed her arms over her chest. "How many meals have you planned?"

"Well, none."

"Then you don't know if it's more difficult or not."

He grinned. "Do you feel better now that you have put me in my place?"

She cracked a smile. "A little."

"If this doesn't work and I have stacks of pink leather left over, it will be your fault."

"It won't come to that. I'm sure of it."

He leaned toward her. "And how many times have you successfully sold leather goods at a farmers market?"

She turned her head slightly to the side. "Never," she mumbled.

He tapped her shoulder to make her look at him. When she did, he cupped his hand around his ear. "I'm sorry, I didn't hear that."

"Going deaf, are you?" He heard the amusement in her voice.

"*Nee*, and I'm not going broke over this project, either. We'll take a small selection and see how it goes."

"Agreed."

"*Goot*, now can we go home? It's getting dark, and soon you won't be able to hear me."

She chuckled. "I'm glad to see you can finally joke about my condition and not worry that you are insulting me."

"Friends do that, right? They tease each other."

"They do. Go ahead, but don't walk so fast. Your legs are longer than mine."

He started toward the house again but stayed by her side. They were back on friendly terms, and he was glad of it. He hadn't ruined their relationship, but he would have to be careful not to be alone with her outside of their work lest he slip up again. It wouldn't take much to prod him into kissing her adorable mouth.

The next morning Gabe's conversation with Esther remained lighthearted and focused on their work together and nothing personal. He wasn't going to make the same mistake twice. After seeing that she had everything she needed to work on, he took the small wagon into Fort Craig. The clinic was busy. He had to wait almost an hour to be seen. Nurse Heather was the one who called him back to the exam room. "How is that arm?" she asked.

"Much better. I did tear a stitch out the day after the doctor put them in."

She scowled at him. "And you didn't come back to see us?"

"It didn't seem worth the trouble of a trip into town. Someone taped it for me."

"I forget that you have to come by horse and buggy. Let me get your vital signs and then we'll have a look."

When she finished her assessment, he rolled up his sleeve. She unwound the bandage. After pressing in several places, she nodded with satisfaction. "It seems to have healed well despite popping a stitch. Once the doctor has a look, I'll remove them and send you on your way. How is Esther? Is she still staying with your family?"

"She is, and she's doing fine. She had a pretty bad headache for a couple of days, but she hasn't complained of anything since."

"I'm glad to hear that. She seemed like a very nice woman."

"You mentioned something about a special kind of hearing aid that your daughters were getting. Is it like a cochlear implant?"

She shook her head. "They are very different, but both do require surgery. Why?"

"Esther had a cochlear implant that didn't work."

She looked surprised. "Really? That's very unusual, but it does happen. How disappointing for her."

"Could she have this other type of hearing aid even if the kind she has failed?"

"As long as she only had a single co-chlear implant, yes. If she had two then the bone-anchored hearing aid isn't an option for her."

"Why?"

"In most instances the patient's own cochlea, an internal part of the ear, is permanently impaired by the implant. Some people have residual hearing after the surgery, but most don't. The bone-anchored device needs an intact cochlea in order to work."

Maybe that was why Esther hadn't been interested in learning about this different type of hearing aid. Because she already knew it wouldn't work for her. But it didn't explain why Nancy had taken a brochure.

The door to the room opened, and the doctor came in. Heather handed him Gabe's chart. "He popped one of the stitches the first day, but the rest look fine," she said.

"How did you manage to do that?" the doctor asked with a sour look.

"Our neighbor's feed wagon broke down. It took several of us to raise it and replace the wheel."

The doctor looked at the nurse with an amused grin. "Remind me to add wheel changing to the list of restricted activities for our next Amish patient."

She nodded solemnly. "Yes, Doctor."

"Go ahead and remove those sutures. Mr. Fisher, it was a pleasure meeting you." He walked out of the room still smiling.

It only took Heather a few minutes to snip the stitches in Gabe's arm. She disposed of the instruments and pulled off her gloves. "You are free to go. Please tell Esther I said hello."

"I'll be sure and do that."

As he paid his bill at the desk, he noticed the stack of information about hearing screens and hearing aids on the counter. He took one about the bone-anchored hearing device to read later. If it wasn't something that would help Esther, he didn't want to bring it up. But if there was a chance that she could be helped, he wanted to learn more about it.

Gabe left the doctor's office and drove to his leather supplier at the edge of town. Ed Carson was a small, bald man with a sour disposition. Gabe didn't hold out much hope that he would have an assortment of colored leather. It turned out that he was wrong. Ed had everything from ivory to deep purple in small quantities. Gabe selected a few and went to pay the man.

"Making pink horse harnesses now?" Ed asked.

"If I could sell them, I'd make them."

"You mentioned last month that you might be wanting a goodly pile of harness leather. I went ahead and tanned some in case you were ready to buy more."

Harness leather wasn't like shoe leather or any other type of leather. It had to be tanned with a lot of oil and waxes to stand up to the elements. "I'm sorry you went to the trouble. My customer decided not to buy from me after all."

"Hank Jefferson, right?"

"That is his name."

"He was in the other day asking who else made harnesses in the area. I gave him a few names. I also told him no one makes them as well as you do."

"I appreciate that."

"Ours are trades that few people value anymore. They want quick and cheap. Pleather instead of real leather. If I can throw any business your way, I will. I admire how the Amish live and work." He bundled up Gabe's purchase and handed it over.

On the trip home, Gabe couldn't help thinking about Esther and how much he wanted to help her. Her last attempt to regain her hearing had failed miserably. There was no guarantee the bone-anchored device would work better for her. He didn't want her to be disappointed again. Nor did he want to suggest she investigate something she already knew wouldn't work. Maybe Waneta was the person he needed to talk with. She would know if Esther had had one or two implants.

When he reached home, he found Esther was bent over her sewing in his workshop. She hadn't noticed him come in. He took care to walk softly across the floor so as not to alert her to his presence by the vibration. He carefully slid the pink leather into her view.

She stopped sewing and looked up with a bright smile. "You found some. This is the exact color I was hoping for. It will make a beautiful purse."

"With a matching dog collar and leash."

"What a good idea."

"I have them sometimes." She wasn't looking at him. He knew he was wasting his breath, but he wanted to say what was on his mind. "I wonder if kissing you would be a good idea or a very bad one," he said softly.

She smoothed the leather with one hand. "This is quite supple. It will be easy to sew." She looked up at him. "Can you cut a few for me now? I'd love to get started on them. Let me finish these ax head covers while you do that."

"I'll get right on it." He took the leather from her and went to his desk. He put the information on the bone-anchored hearing aid in the top drawer. One day soon, when this rush of work was over, he would talk to Esther about it. It might not be something her family could afford or that her church would consider paying for, but he would help if it meant she could hear again. He closed the drawer and stepped to his cutting table. It wasn't long before he deposited the new purse pieces in front of her.

"*Danki.* It will just take me another minute to finish this," she said, looking up at him.

"All right. I'm going to the house."

"Okay. Send Pamela out. I need to speak to her about the patterns for the lining I want."

"I'll do that."

Gabe found all the women in his mother's quilting room. He gave Pamela Esther's message and then looked at Waneta. "May I speak to you for a few moments?"

"Of course." She got up from her chair beside the quilting frame and followed him into the kitchen. "Has Esther become a problem?"

He frowned. "*Nee*, nothing like that."

"Then how may I help you?"

"Esther told me that her cochlear implant failed."

"So she claims."

"You don't believe that?"

"Her father doesn't. He thinks she refuses to use it so she can continue her work with deaf children at the special-needs school. Some of the deaf teachers there are not Amish. They are proud of being deaf. They don't believe deafness is something that needs to be corrected."

"It is decided by *Gott* that they should be as they are."

"It is His will, to be sure, but we are not prevented by our faith from seeking medical cures for our children when they have an illness. Esther's parents sought a cure for her disability that she felt she didn't need. They sacrificed a great deal to get her surgery. In her father's eyes, she is being selfish by refusing to use it. I agree with him. She could have been happily married with children of her own by now. Something her father and I dearly want to see. I went to great lengths to encourage a match for her. We would have made her husband a half owner in our bakery. All she had to do was learn to live with the sounds the device allowed her to hear. Perhaps it isn't perfect, but it has to be better than nothing."

There were always two sides to a story. This was Waneta's view. Esther's refusal to marry Waneta's choice was at the heart of the hard feelings between them. Should he tell Waneta he agreed with Esther? A man who would court a deaf woman in order to gain ownership in a business wasn't much of a catch.

Gabe drew a deep breath. He was being unfair to the man. He could have had deep feelings for Esther. She was an easy woman to love.

"I'm sorry the two of you have remained at odds over her decision, but it is her life. Because she is deaf doesn't mean she had to settle for a man she believed didn't love her."

Waneta looked affronted, but she simply folded her arms over her chest. "What is it you wanted to ask me?"

"Did Esther have two cochlear implants or only one?"

"One was deemed enough by her doctor."

"*Danki.* I want you to know she isn't a problem for me. She works very hard and she has some *goot* ideas about growing my business. With her help I'm sure I can produce enough items to make having a booth at the festival worthwhile."

"It's a shame she won't be there to see your success or the lack of it."

"Why wouldn't she attend the festival? Are you leaving sooner than planned?"

"We aren't. She is."

# Chapter Twelve

Esther looked up from her sewing machine when Gabe came in. She knew at once that he was upset by the expression on his face. "What's wrong?"

He walked over to lean against the cutting table and crossed his arms over his chest as he faced her. "You're leaving."

"You knew that."

"I didn't know you were leaving in five days."

She pushed her chair back and clasped her hands together in her lap. "Who told you?"

"Does it matter?"

"Waneta?"

"Is it true?"

"I didn't want to come on this trip. My father insisted. The woman he hired to drive us out here went on to stay with some family in Bar Harbor for several weeks. She agreed that when she was ready to drive back to Ohio, she would take any of us who wanted to go along with her. I was delighted to learn of her offer. I thought two weeks would be more than enough time to satisfy my father. However, that was before I became involved with you and your work."

"Then I don't understand."

"Waneta called Bessie and then wrote to my father to tell him I was coming home. I never said I wanted to leave so soon. I didn't agree to go. I like to finish what I start, Gabe."

Some of the tenseness left his body. "So you aren't leaving before the Potato Blossom Festival."

"I want to see you succeed. I think *Gott* has given you a wonderful talent and more people should know about the things you create. I'm sorry if Waneta upset you. I will make it clear to her that I am not going home until she and my sisters are ready to go."

A half smile pulled up the corner of his mouth. "I can't tell you how relieved that makes me. I've gotten used to having you around."

She grinned. "The feeling is mutual."

"I guess we can get back to work now. What did Pamela say about the linings?"

"She can have three of them ready for us by tomorrow morning. It won't take me long to stitch them in."

"Then I had better get busy cutting more leather. How do you say that in ASL?"

"Say what?"

"Get busy."

She giggled and showed him. He repeated the motion. She nodded and turned back to her machine.

He tapped her shoulder. "Thank you," he signed, surprising her.

"Has Jonah been teaching you more sign language?"

"A little. Not good yet."

Her heart swelled with gratitude for Gabe's kindness and willingness to learn to communicate with her. Every day she discovered something about him that made him dearer to her. When she did finally leave Maine, she was going to miss him dreadfully.

Esther and Gabe worked long into the evening that night and started again early the next morning. After they finished, she had a conversation with Waneta to let her know she wasn't going to leave with Bessie. She had been surprised when Waneta didn't object.

Now, late in the afternoon, Esther's eyes were scratchy from staring at the sewing needle for hours on end. Her back ached from leaning over the machine, but she was finished. It was time to pack up their items for the trip into town in the morning. She looked around the workshop with a sense of great satisfaction. They had accomplished a lot together.

Gabe stood in front of her. "Tired?"

"A little," she said and signed the same.

His signing was improving. Jonah had told her that Gabe sent away for a book on ASL so he could continue to study it even after they went back to Ohio. It was one thing to memorize the signs. It was another thing to be able to communicate effortlessly. Unless Gabe had someone he could practice with, he wouldn't become fluent. She didn't tell him that. He was so pleased with what he had learned.

Daily he demonstrated a new phrase or two that he had mastered. She adored helping him. It was cute watching him try, fail sometimes and then try harder. He had an aptitude for it that surprised her. She had started signing whenever she spoke to him to help him learn.

Suddenly he winced. "We don't need that."

"What?"

"Thunder. The forecast said there was a chance of storms tonight and for tomorrow."

"*Nee*. It can't rain tomorrow." They had

worked so hard to get ready. If it rained, few if any people would come to the market.

He looked at the ceiling. "I don't know about tomorrow, but it's raining now. I hear it on the roof."

She looked up, too. "I remember what that sounded like. Soothing. It meant we wouldn't be working in the fields the next day."

"The crops need rain. We shouldn't wish it away."

"Can we pray for a pause from ten o'clock to four o'clock tomorrow?"

"I think that will be acceptable. Are you ready to make a dash to the house?"

"I won't melt."

"You won't? Aren't you sugar and spice and everything nice?" His words were teasing, but his expression became oddly serious.

"You are confusing me with my sisters." She grew warm beneath his intense scrutiny.

He tugged gently on her *kapp* ribbon.

"I think not. They may be sweet, but I haven't seen a sign of spice among them."

"Sweet is usually enough for most young men."

He didn't take his eyes off her face. "Not me. I like spicy."

She knew she was blushing. "We should go to the house before the storm gets worse."

He took a step back. "You're right."

She quickly headed for the door. When she opened it, the rain was coming down in sheets. Gabe caught her by the shoulder. She turned to see him holding a large piece of hide.

"I don't have an umbrella, but this should work. Stay close to me."

She nodded. He held the hide over his head and stepped out. She pressed against his side to keep from getting wet as they rushed toward the front porch of the house, but she stumbled and fell to her knees. Gabe lifted her up and kept one arm around her. He couldn't control the hide with one hand. The wind carried the rain into her face in spite of his efforts to keep her dry. Her *kapp* and her hem were soaked by the time they reached cover.

She laughed as she ran up the steps and shook out her dress. Gabe dropped the hide on the porch floor. He pulled a handkerchief from his pocket and began to mop her face. "I didn't help much."

They stood close together. His hand stilled. She saw his eyes darken. She couldn't look away from him. She didn't want to.

Why hadn't she realized it before now? She was halfway to falling in love with this wonderful man.

He leaned toward her. She knew he was going to kiss her. She raised her face and closed her eyes.

His lips touched hers. Gently. As softly as a rose petal, and then they were gone. Her heart began racing as her breath caught in her throat. His hands settled on her shoulders. Nothing mattered except being closer to him. She pressed her hands to his chest and leaned against him as his arms circled her and drew her near. She wanted to keep kissing him.

Part of Gabe's mind said he was making a mistake. There would be no going back from this, but he was past caring. She was in his arms. He wanted to hold her forever. Her lips were as sweet as honeysuckle nectar. One kiss would never be enough. She was everything he'd ever wanted and never knew he needed.

The sound of the door opening behind him brought reality crashing back into view. He glanced over his shoulder. His father stood in the doorway. "I saw you running through the rain, but then you didn't come in. Is everything all right?"

"It's fine. We'll be a minute."

"Okay." His father appeared puzzled, but he went back inside and closed the door.

Gabe looked down at Esther. Her eyes were filled with confusion as she gazed at him. He nodded toward the door. "My father wanted to know if we were all right."

She pressed a hand to her cheek. "He saw us? You—me?"

"Did he see me kiss you? I don't think so."

"I'm so embarrassed. How will I face him?"

"Like nothing happened except that you got wet and took a moment to dry your face with my kerchief." He pressed the damp cloth into her hand. "Go in. The longer we stand out here, the stranger it will look."

"What? I didn't catch all that you said."

"Dry your face and go in."

She stepped around him and looked back. There was so much he wanted to say to her. He didn't know where to start, and this wasn't the time to sort it out. "Go."

She went inside. He picked up the wet hide and shook it off. A moment later he opened the door and leaned in. "*Mamm*, have you got something I can use to dry this piece of leather? I don't want the water to stain it."

His mother appeared with a dish towel. "Will this work?"

"Great. *Danki.*"

"Is Esther okay? She ran upstairs without a word."

"I'm sure she just wanted to get out of her wet things. She slipped and fell."

"Oh, the poor child. I'll fix some hot tea for her. And for you. You look like you need it."

"Sounds *goot*."

She made a tsking sound. "The two of you have been working entirely too hard."

"I don't think we'll be putting in any more long hours." He began to dry the leather he'd used as an ineffective umbrella. He couldn't be sure Esther would want to see him again, let alone work beside him. Why hadn't he kept his feelings under wraps?

Because of the way she had looked at him. With such wonder in her eyes. Like she had discovered a new rare flower.

She wasn't indifferent to him. But what did it really mean? She would be leaving. Not in a few days but in a few weeks with her family. She had made no secret of the fact that she wouldn't marry a hearing man. Where did that leave him? Was it possible he could change her mind?

"What are Seth and Asher doing?"

Gabe followed his mother's gaze. His brothers were standing in the barn door. When they saw they had his attention, they beckoned to him.

His heart sank. Something told him his interlude with Esther hadn't gone unnoticed after all. He managed a half-hearted smile for his mother and handed her the towel. "I'll go see what they want."

"Don't stay out there long. Supper will be ready in half an hour." She smiled, patted his cheek the way she had done since he was a child and went in.

Gabe dashed across to the open barn door. Asher and Seth took a step back to let him inside. He shook the rain from his hat. "What do you fellows want?"

"An explanation would be nice," Seth said.

"About what?"

"Don't play coy," Asher grumbled.

"Okay. I suspect you saw me kiss Esther. What do you want to know?"

Seth planted his hands on his hips. "Your intentions, for one thing? Please tell me you aren't just feeling sorry for her. That would not be fair to her."

"I haven't had time to sort out how I feel. What are your intentions toward Pamela?"

"Don't change the subject," Seth snapped, then he took a deep breath. "Pamela and I are walking out together. I may be courting her in earnest before they leave. We get along amazingly well. Your turn."

"Esther and I have been working long hours, and I think the strain got to us. We finished enough pieces to take to the farmers market tomorrow, and the relief went to my head. Maybe to hers, too. I didn't intend to kiss her—it just happened."

"Now that it has, what next?" Asher asked. "You are the one who warned us that Waneta was intent on getting husbands for the girls while they were here. Are you sure you aren't being manipulated?"

Gabe scoffed at the idea. "*Nee*, Esther doesn't want me for a husband."

Asher gave him a hard look. "What makes you say that?"

"Because I'm not deaf. She believes only a deaf man can understand all that she endures and enjoys in her silent world."

Seth laid a hand on Gabe's shoulder. "I think it's time the two of you revisited that assumption, because she didn't look like she cared if you could hear or not."

"I'd love to have that conversation, but I'm not sure I can make her understand all that I want to tell her."

Esther sat on the edge of her bed in her damp clothing. She had one hand pressed to her mouth as if she could hold on to the feeling of Gabe's lips against hers. Why had he kissed her? Why had she let him? They were so wrong for each other. How, then, could a kiss feel so right? It had been perfect in every way. Her heart soared at the memory and then plunged to the pit of her stomach when she realized she had no idea what to do next.

She was startled when Julia sat down on the cot across from hers. "What's the matter?" she signed.

Esther took one look at her sister's concerned face and burst into tears. Julia moved to Esther's side and gathered her close, patting her back until Esther's sobs abated. Esther scrubbed away her tears with both hands. "I'm sorry I'm being so silly."

"Gabe?" Julia signed.

Esther didn't question how Julia had guessed the cause of her distress. She simply nodded.

Julia took both of Esther's hands in her own and leaned forward to make sure Esther could see her. "Tell me."

"He kissed me."

"Was it awful?"

"It was wonderful."

Julia sat back with a puzzled expression on her face. "Then why the tears?" she signed.

"He's not the man I want to be in love with," she said.

"Who is?" Julia signed.

"I don't know, but Gabe shouldn't be the one who makes my heart beat faster."

Julia shook her head. "Esther, you are not the one who decides that."

"What do you mean?"

"*Gott* decides our partners for life. He chooses. We can say yes or no to that decision. We have free will, but surely we must put our faith in His plan for us if we are to live as He desires."

"I'm so confused. I don't know what to do or what to say to Gabe now."

"Foolish little sister. One kiss does not mean you must marry him. It means the two of you are drawn to each other. Give yourself a chance to see if he is the right one or not. Open your heart to *Gott's* plan. Don't turn your back on it because it isn't the path you think you want."

"How do I face him?"

"I would suggest you start by changing into dry clothes and then come down for supper the way you always have."

"You mean pretend the kiss didn't happen?"

"I mean act like it isn't the end of the world or the end of your friendship with Gabe. See what he has to say with an open mind. I know you like him."

"I think I'm falling in love with him."

"Then give him a chance. The two of you have worked very hard to make a success of his business. Don't let him down now."

Esther nodded and then threw her arms around her sister. "You're so wise. How did you get that way?" She drew back to look at Julia's face.

"Trial and error."

"I saw you with Danny Coblentz Sunday evening. Do you like him?"

Julia's eyes suddenly snapped with anger. "Not in the least."

Shocked, Esther laid a hand on Julia's arm. "What happened?"

"I discovered that we aren't suited.

Nancy and Pamela seem to have found happiness here. Waneta will have to be content with that." She stood and left the room.

Esther chided herself for being wrapped up in her own feelings and not paying more attention to her sister. She had often accused her siblings of the same thing. It wasn't gratifying to discover she had the same flaw.

After changing, she went downstairs in time to see everyone heading into the kitchen. She took a deep breath and squared her shoulders. She would act like it wasn't the end of the world or of her friendship with Gabe. She could do that.

Maybe.

She went into the kitchen and took her place at the table opposite Gabe. She forced herself to smile. Everyone bowed their heads to pray except for him.

"Are you okay?" he signed.

She kept her smile in place. "I am. Thank you." She folded her hands and closed her eyes.

After a minute, Nancy nudged her to signal the prayer had ended. Esther kept her eyes on her plate for the rest of the meal, ignoring any conversation that might have gone on.

After the meal ended, the men filed out of the kitchen and into the living room. The women made quick work of the dishes and the cleanup and soon followed the men. Nancy went to sit beside Moses. Pamela and Seth joined the couple, where they began playing a board game pitting the boys against the girls. Asher was reading. Zeke had a book beside him but was dozing in his favorite chair. Julia was stitching another purse lining. Waneta and Talitha were both knitting and conversing at a small table in the corner. Gabe sat by the window with Jonah perched beside him on the arm of his chair. There was nowhere left for her to sit except across from Gabe.

*Act like it's not the end of the world or the end of our friendship*, she repeated to herself and sat in the chair. There was a book on birds beside it. She opened it and began reading about the birds of Florida. After a few minutes, she glanced up to find Gabe staring at her.

"Jonah, teach me some new words. What is the sign for 'I apologize' or 'I'm sorry'?"

"That's an easy one. Close your fist with your thumb outside. It's also the letter *A*. Bring your hand to your chest and make several circles." Jonah demonstrated. Gabe took his time making the gesture slowly.

Gabe repeated it several times while keeping his gaze fixed on Esther. "What about 'please forgive me'?"

Jonah glanced between Gabe and Esther as if he wasn't sure what was going on. "Hold one hand palm up and stroke it away from yourself with the tips of the fingers on your other hand. Like this."

"How do I say, 'you're forgiven'?" Gabe asked, looking at Esther.

"You're forgiven," Esther signed before Jonah could show him.

Jonah frowned at her. "Gabe asked me to teach him," he signed quickly.

"Then I am sorry, too," she said softly and signed it.

A faint smile curved Gabe's lips as he nodded slightly in her direction. "Jonah, show me how to say, 'we should talk about it tomorrow.'"

She focused on the book she held, refusing to think about the way his lips had touched hers only a little while ago. "Gabe, did you know that flamingos are gray but they turn pink because of a natural pink dye called can-thax-an-thin? I think that's how you say it. They get it from the brine shrimp and blue-green algae they eat."

She glanced at him. His grin widened. "I did."

She went back to her book. "Birds are interesting creatures." She slanted a glance his way.

"Almost as unique as flowers." He held her sketch pad toward her. "You forgot this in the garden. I brought it in last night."

"Thank you for rescuing it before the rain."

"Do you have any new sketches for leather decorations in here?"

"Actually, I do."

"May I see them?"

She scooted her chair closer to him, took the sketch pad and opened it. She skipped past the drawings of his mouth, but she was sure she was blushing, anyway. When she reached the drawings she'd made of the roses, she held the book for him to see a couple of the items that she had envisioned. "I thought a single rose on a leather key chain might be something that would sell."

He considered it for a few seconds and then nodded. "I like the idea." Then he signed, "We should talk about it tomorrow."

Esther was sure he didn't mean her sketches.

# Chapter Thirteen

Esther didn't sleep much that night. She woke early and went downstairs to the kitchen. Gabe was the only other person up. He had the coffee can and the percolator in front of him by the sink.

"Let me do that," she said.

He stepped aside. She couldn't bring herself to look at his face. She was too nervous about what he would say. She couldn't bear it if he said he regretted kissing her. She would treasure the memory of those few moments for the rest of her life.

After spooning in the grounds and setting the percolator on the stove, she finally faced him. He was sitting at the table in his usual place turning an empty coffee mug around and around in his hands. He looked more nervous than she felt. In that moment she took pity on him. She hadn't considered that this might be difficult for him, too.

Pulling out her chair, she sat down, propped her elbows on the table and rested her chin on her hands. "I believe it is tomorrow. Did you have something you wanted to say?"

"I had it all rehearsed in my head, but sitting across from you now, I realize that is not what I really wanted to tell you."

"Gabe, it was a nice kiss. Plain and simple."

His eyebrows shot up. "I thought you would be angry with me."

"Surprised, but not angry. As someone recently reminded me, a kiss does not mean we are going to get married. If you are worried that I am expecting a proposal this morning, I can assure you that I'm not."

"I honestly didn't know what I thought you were expecting from me today. I care for you a lot, Esther."

"And I feel the same. You have become a very dear friend. If we let it, a simple kiss could make things awkward between us. I don't want that."

"I wouldn't call it a simple kiss."

She crossed her arms on the tabletop. Didn't he realize he was making it harder for her? "It was short but sweet."

"You're being very mature about this."

She was glad he thought so, because she wasn't feeling that way. She was shaking on the inside. "I could wring my hands and wail if you want." Oh, so easily.

Gabe relaxed for the first time since he'd left the barn with his brothers the night before. "*Nee.* I'm pleased with your attitude. I got carried away yesterday. I'm not going to say that I regret it, because I don't. I won't lie to you. I've thought about it more than once. You are a very attractive woman. But you are also my friend, and the last thing I want is for my lack of self-control to jeopardize that friendship."

She remained silent, and he wasn't sure why. "Did you understand what I said?"

"You start talking too fast when you have a lot to say. I got most of it."

"I could write it down for you if you'd like."

"I think the important part was that you don't want what happened to affect our friendship. Am I right?"

He thought the main point was that he'd considered kissing her before. Either she hadn't understood that part or she was choosing to ignore it. Whichever it was, he'd probably do best to follow her lead. "Absolutely."

She nodded and stood up. "Then we won't let it affect us. We still have some work to do to get ready for the farmers market today. We need to price the items and then pack them. We need to take enough money to make change and something for lunch, unless you want to eat at the market. Is there anything else?"

He held up his empty cup. "Can I get some coffee first?"

She grinned. "I reckon you may."

She took his cup and moved to the stove.

Gabe let out a sigh of relief. The morning was turning out so much better than he'd expected. Esther wasn't angry with him. She still intended to help him with his business, and he was going to have the pleasure of her company until she and her family left Maine after the Potato Blossom Festival. It was more than he deserved.

The one thing that nagged at him was how easily she dismissed the moment they'd shared as a simple kiss. For him it had been anything but simple. Perhaps she didn't care for him the way he'd hoped she would. As a friend, yes, but he wanted to be more to her.

It didn't take them long to price and load his merchandise. Because it was his first time at the market, he had no idea how much he could reasonably expect to sell. Taking a lot might mean coming home with a lot, and he didn't want that. He still had his hopes pinned on the festival to generate the most income, but Esther was right. He couldn't depend on a single event to maintain his business. If Jefferson had purchased the harnesses he had talked about, it would've made all the difference. Instead Gabe was left trying to nickel and dime his way through his family's financial difficulties.

After loading the boxes in the back of the small wagon, Gabe climbed up and held his hand out to assist Esther. She hesitated, and his spirits sank. While she might claim their kiss hadn't affected their friendship, he could see that it had.

She took a step back. "I almost forgot my sketchbook."

She hurried to the house and returned a few minutes later with her quilted satchel over her shoulder. She smiled up at him and held out her hand.

"I doubt you will find any wildflowers to draw," he said.

"Perhaps not, but I can show customers

other items we can make for them and even how we might personalize them."

He happily took her hand and helped her up. If his venture was a success, it would be due to her business savvy and determination.

The trip into Fort Craig took nearly an hour. He had decided to drive one of the draft horses. Olive was a dappled gray Percheron. She wasn't as fleet of foot as Topper, but she was impressive wearing the parade harness he had made for Jefferson. The more people who saw Gabe's work, the more likely he was to find a customer for the piece.

The area set aside for the market was in the parking lot of a restaurant that had closed several years before. When they reached it, Gabe saw there were already dozens of folding tables covered in red checkered tablecloths arranged around the perimeter along with tents and wagons. There were signs for everything—straw bales, seasonal vegetables, local pork products, honey, eggs, herbs, flowers, baked goods, handmade jewelry and even fresh-brewed coffee.

He stopped Olive beside Michael Shetler's tent. Olive pawed the pavement with her huge steel-shod hooves, making a loud clatter. When she tossed her head, the bright diamond-shaped chrome dots on her bridle flashed in the sunlight. It wasn't long before she began drawing admirers.

Michael and Bethany stepped out of their tent. "I confess I'm a little jealous, Gabe. I wish I had a clock the size of your horse to advertise my merchandise."

Gabe chuckled. "She is more fidgety than our other horses. I thought her color would show off the harness nicely."

"It does."

Bethany helped Esther down from the wagon seat. "Welcome to our farmers market."

Gabe was pleased to note that his friend's wife was speaking slowly and looking directly at Esther. He wanted Esther to feel comfortable in an unfamiliar place. He needn't have worried. She and Bethany went straight to the flower stand.

Michael helped Gabe get his makeshift table of hay bales and wide boards set up beside the wagon. Esther returned with several small pots of flowers. "I thought your mother might like these for her garden."

"That's very thoughtful. I'm sure she will. Do you feel uneasy working beside me?"

"Gabe, I already told you that what happened isn't going to make a difference in our friendship."

He shoved his hands in his pockets. "That's not what I meant. Are you going to be comfortable dealing with customers?"

"Oh." Her cheeks blossomed bright red. "Of course. I will just make sure people know that I'm deaf and that I have to read their lips. I must warn you that many of them will shout at me when they learn that. You may have to learn to ignore it."

"Thanks for the warning."

Olive did her job of attracting people to Gabe's area. He spent more time letting children and adults pet her and answering their questions than selling his leather pieces. Esther did the bulk of the work behind the table. A few times he had to step in when she couldn't understand what the customer was asking. The men with bushy beards she couldn't read at all, but for the most part she did well without Gabe's assistance.

They had been at the market for almost two hours when he heard a familiar voice. "Mr. Fisher. How nice to see you."

Heather, the nurse from the clinic, came up to the table with a group of kids and adults. She smiled at Esther. "This is my husband, Randy, and our children, Frank, Carmen and Sophie. These women are Polly and Frances Minor. Friends from the School for the Deaf in Portland. They're visiting our hobby farm this week," she said as she signed.

The little boy tugged on her skirt and signed something. Heather nodded.

Esther came around from behind the table, knelt in front of the children and began signing. Her smile was bright, her motions larger and more energetic than Gabe had seen before. It was as if she had suddenly been let out of a small box. The women with Heather were equally animated and fluid in their signing. In that moment he realized ASL was a true language, not simply a string of hand motions. Even with her sisters she wasn't this expressive. Her family was always reserved when signing.

Esther rose to her feet and looked at him. Her expression was joyful. She was in her element. He was the one on the outside looking in.

"Frank would like to meet Olive, if that's okay."

"Tell him that's fine. Come along and I'll introduce you."

Esther quickly signed his reply, and the little boy beamed with delight. Randy took the boy's hand and followed Gabe to where the mare was dozing. Gabe picked up the boy and spoke softly to Olive. She reached out to nuzzle Frank's arm. He drew back in fright. "*Nee,* it's okay. That's how she gets to know you," Gabe said.

The boy turned to his father, who signed Gabe's reassurance. The child nodded and held out his hand. His grin widened as the horse touched him with her lips. He pulled his hand away, but he was still smiling.

Gabe glanced at Randy. "Would it be okay if I put him on Olive's back?"

"Sure." The man signed for the boy, who clapped eagerly.

Gabe settled the child and showed him how to hold on to Olive's harness. The boy made a quick motion with his hands. Gabe turned to his father.

Randy chuckled. "He wants to go for a ride."

"Would your daughters like to join him?" Gabe glanced at the girls, who were standing with downcast faces.

"I'll ask." Frank signed to them, and they dashed toward Gabe.

He held up his hand to stop them. "Don't run near a horse. It can frighten them."

"Okay." The one with a pink headband signed to her sister. She turned and held up her arms to Gabe. "I'm Sophie. This is Carmen. She's deaf."

Gabe lifted Sophie to Olive's back behind Frank and noticed the girl's headband had one of the hearing aids attached to it. The second little girl wasn't wearing one.

With Randy walking beside the children, Gabe led them on a circuit around the parking lot. Olive had given up her fidgeting and walked patiently and carefully. She knew she had children on her back.

When the ride was over, Gabe and Randy lowered the kids to the ground. They hurried away to their mother, where they vied with each other to tell the story in sign for her.

"Thanks, that was kind of you," Randy said.

"You are blessed. Children are *Gott's* most marvelous gift to us."

"I am, although some people wouldn't see three hearing-impaired children as a blessing."

Gabe nodded solemnly. "Those are the people in most need of our prayers, for they are blind in the spiritual sense no matter how good their eyesight is. Can I ask you a question about Sophie?"

"You are wondering why she wears a hearing aid and Carmen doesn't. Heather mentioned you had questions about the same kind of device for Esther."

"*Ja.*"

"Carmen couldn't get used to being bombarded with sounds after being deaf for four years. She found it distressing. It may be a reaction to the neglect she suffered. To her, silence may be better than the screaming, shouting and fighting she witnessed when she was with her mother. We can't be sure. She is happier not hearing. Heather and I are comfortable with her choice. Frank will never hear. He was born without the nerve that connects his inner ear to his brain. No hearing aid can help him. We are a blended family in more ways than one."

"*Danki*—thank you."

"Sure. I do have to say you may have ruined my son's upcoming birthday."

Gabe frowned. "How so?"

"My wife and I are getting a pony for the kids. He may not measure up to Olive in their eyes."

Gabe laughed. "A horse of their own is a fine gift that they will soon love. They are welcome to come see Olive anytime they want a ride on a giant again."

"I'll tell them."

Sophie dashed toward them but slowed a few feet away and walked slowly to Gabe. "Mommy says you and Esther are invited to Frank's birthday party on Friday. Can you come?"

"Tell your mother I thank her for the invitation."

"Can you bring Olive?" Sophie asked hopefully.

Gabe glanced at Randy, smothered a smile and shook his head. "Olive will be busy working that day. My brothers are cutting wood for the winter, and she must pull the big logs with her sister Honey."

"Oh. Well, you can still come. You really have two giant horses?"

"My family owns six draft horses, plus two ordinary ones that pull our buggy."

"It must be nice to be Amish. We don't even have one horse. But we do have a dog." She turned and went back to her siblings.

Randy patted Olive's shoulder. "That's a fine harness Olive is wearing. Did you make it?"

"I did. That's my main business."

"I've been thinking about having our pony trained to pull a cart for the children. Can you recommend a trainer?"

"My brother Asher. Olive is an example of his success. We bought her as an untrained two-year-old. She's four now. You can see how well she turned out. I'm sure Asher would be interested in training your pony."

"Great. How do I get ahold of him if I decide to go that route?"

"We have an answering machine in the phone booth we share with our Amish neighbors. You can leave a message there." Gabe gave him the number, and Randy typed it into his cell phone.

"Esther appears to be in a spirited conversation with the teachers from the School for the Deaf," Gabe said. "I've seen her using ASL with her family, but it isn't like that."

"Are her other family members deaf?"

"They aren't."

"I've read that the Amish speak their own language called Pennsylvania Dutch. Is that true?"

"It is. We call it Pennsylvania *Deitsh* or just *Deitsh*. I learned *Englisch* when I started school, as do most Amish children."

"Do you speak more freely in *Deitsh*?"

"I do. I have to think about my *Englisch* words."

"It's the same with ASL. If you use it every day, all day long, it becomes second nature. If you only use it when the deaf family member is in the room, you need to think about what you are signing. It doesn't come naturally." Randy walked back to join his wife.

As Gabe watched Esther, he wondered if his attempts to sign amused her. He was little more than a toddler uttering his first words compared to the people she was talking to now. She was like one of the wild birds he liked to watch. She was freely fluttering her wings in the sunshine. Her song was one that only another deaf person could hear.

No matter how hard he studied sign language, it would take him years to become so accomplished. How much of what he wanted to tell her would remain unsaid or missed? He tried to imagine being married to her. How would he speak to her in the night?

Now he saw why she wanted a deaf spouse. She deserved a man she could understand and converse with easily. A man she didn't have to try to guess at what he was saying.

He cared deeply for her, but was that enough? Unless there was a hearing device that worked for her, Gabe wasn't sure he could sway her to consider him or that he should try. He wanted more than the half life she had with him now.

By the time the market closed at four o'clock, Esther had helped sell almost all of the merchandise she and Gabe had brought with them. She was delighted that her pink purses with their flowered borders had sold out, and she had orders for six more in different colors. When they finished packing up and headed for home, Esther realized that Gabe had been very quiet for the past few hours.

"We did well today," she said, looking for his reaction.

He merely nodded.

"I have orders for a half dozen more purses."

He glanced her way. "That's good."

"This trip to the farmers market was a success. And yet you don't seem happy."

That drew his attention. "Of course I'm happy."

"So what is on your mind?"

He shrugged. "Nothing in particular."

"There must be, because you don't usually snub me."

He looked startled. "I'm not snubbing you. I had a nice day. I saw you had a wonderful time with your new friends."

"Is that why you are upset? Because I made new friends?"

"Of course not." He didn't say anything else.

She studied his profile as he kept his eyes straight ahead, but she couldn't drop the issue.

"Yesterday you kissed me, and this afternoon you can barely look at me. Are the two related?"

He turned Olive off the highway onto a

patch of grass and stopped. He twisted in his seat to look at Esther.

"Maybe they are related. Today I saw you as you truly are."

"I don't know what you mean."

"I saw you excited to be with people like yourself."

"Deaf people." She crossed her arms against the chill that suddenly struck her. "You didn't like what you saw."

"*Nee*, that's just it. I loved what I saw. I've never seen you so comfortable and happy. Watching you I realized you are always focused on trying to understand what is being said by me and others. I thought your intense concentration was just part of who you are. I didn't realize it was part of your struggle. Jonah told me speech-reading is hard, but I didn't realize how much effort you put into it until today. With those people, you didn't have to work at understanding them. It was amazing to see."

She had no idea what to say. After a few moments, he got the horse moving again.

She traveled beside him in silence wondering how his revelation would change things between them, because she sensed that it had. When they reached his home, he carried the leftover merchandise back in the shop and set the box on his desk.

"Are we going to work this evening?" she asked.

He shook his head and then turned around. "I must help my father and brothers cut wood. They are working down along the river. I'll join them shortly. I'd like you to make a few dozen more purses and key chains. Those were popular."

She didn't want him to leave with this strain between them. "It was nice of you to give Heather's children a ride on Olive."

A smile tugged at the corner of his mouth. "I liked Heather's *kinder* and her husband."

"Are you going to Frank's birthday party?"

"Maybe. Will you go?"

"I'd love to, if you wouldn't mind taking me. I don't like to drive."

"I did not know that. Of course I'll take you."

"*Danki*. Gabe, are we okay?"

"Sure."

"I'm not any different than I was two days ago."

He pressed his lips into a tight line and nodded. "Maybe I am. I want you to be happy. You know that, don't you?"

She gestured around the room. "Well, this makes me happy."

He pushed away from the desk. "That's good, because we have a lot more work to do."

After he left, Esther set about cutting out several more patterns. She had been working for about half an hour when the outside door opened. Mr. Jefferson walked in. He scanned the room. "Where's Gabe?"

"Down at the river, cutting wood. If you would like to leave a message, I think I have a pen and paper here somewhere."

She opened her satchel, searched for a suitable piece of paper and then pulled it out along with a pencil. When she looked up, Jefferson was walking out.

"So no message?" she signed in annoyance.

She walked to the door to look out and saw him driving away. Shrugging off his brusque manner, she went back to work.

That evening after supper, she sat on the sofa putting the finishing touches on a new dress. Jonah walked by with the book of sign language that had come in the mail for Gabe that day and carried it to him. She couldn't see what Jonah was saying, but she imagined he was asking Gabe if he wanted to learn some new signs.

Gabe shook his head, took the book from Jonah and laid it aside. "Let's play a game of checkers instead."

"Mr. Jefferson stopped by," she said. "Did he find you?"

Jonah turned to her. "Gabe wants to know what he wanted."

"He didn't say. He just left."

Gabe never even glanced at her.

Esther focused on her needlework again. Something had changed today. In her heart she knew they weren't okay.

# Chapter Fourteen

Esther was glad when Gabe left to cut
wood again after lunch. Their morning work had kept them both busy. They
found little time to speak to each other. Or
rather, they had avoided speaking to one
another. She didn't understand it. Had his
amazing kiss meant nothing?

If he wasn't upset that she had made
new friends, what was the issue? Had
she somehow offended him? It wasn't
like Gabe to be so withdrawn. They had
been able to talk about almost anything.
Why couldn't he tell her what was wrong?

Should she press him when he returned? She wasn't sure what she should do.

She was cleaning up the leather scraps from around his cutting table when Julia came in.

"I came to let you know that I'm leaving with Bessie on Saturday," she signed.

Esther set her broom aside. "Why?"

"I'm ready to go home."

"Is it because of Danny?"

Julia nodded. "He came to see me yesterday. I told him not to come back. I think the best thing is to leave before he does."

"Sister, you must tell me what's going on."

"You know I rejected Ogden Martin's proposal last fall, but you don't know everything. I tried to let him down gently, but he was persistent. He followed me wherever I went, to town, to visit friends. The worst of it was when his parents came to chastise me for treating their son so poorly."

"I knew they came to see you. I didn't realize that was why."

"Ogden cornered me in the grocery store a few days later to tell me I had broken his mother's heart. It was the last straw. I told him to stay away from me or the bishop would hear about his behavior. I honestly never thought I would have to do that, but when Ogden stopped me on the road a few days later, I felt I had no choice. The bishop was sympathetic to me. I had feared he would take Ogden's side, but he went to Ogden's home to speak to him. Ogden's parents were mortified, but at least he finally stopped bothering me."

**"What does that have to do with Danny? Is he behaving poorly?"**

"Danny and Ogden are cousins who were very close when they were young. Ogden wrote Danny to tell him I would be visiting the Fishers. Danny sought me out here to find out if I was as heartless as Ogden said and to ask why I treated him so badly. I foolishly thought it was because he liked me."

**"He didn't say that, did he?"** Esther was

shocked. Danny had seemed like such a nice man, though she had only met him briefly.

"Danny has his mind made up about me. I am not going to try to change it. So I'm leaving."

"Julia, I'm so sorry."

"Don't be. I believe the Lord is leading me toward a single life. I will be the doting *aenti* for Nancy and Pamela's children. And for yours."

"You will be a wonderful *aenti*. Clearly, Danny is a fool if he can't see what a sweet person you are."

"What about you? Are you ready to go home? You looked so glum at breakfast this morning."

Maybe that was what she was supposed to do—go home. Gabe would have to manage his business alone, but she had done a lot to improve his chances of success. "I'm not sure what I should do. Part of me wants to stay here until after the festival. Another part of me says there isn't much point." Not unless something changed.

"I would dearly love to have your company on the trip home."

"I'll consider it." She gave her sister a hug. "I will miss you, even if it's only for a short time."

Julia drew back and signed, "I will miss you, too."

After Julia left, Esther sat down at the sewing machine. It didn't seem fair that her oldest sister's hopes for marriage and motherhood had been dashed by two men in the same family. Danny was a friend of Gabe's. Would Gabe intervene if Esther told him what Julia said?

After five hours spent with a chain saw, Gabe was happy to finally get the wood chips and sawdust out of his hair. As he stepped out of the bathroom after washing up, he almost ran into Nancy as she came bouncing down the hall.

"Have you seen Moses?" she asked cheerfully.

"He's bringing up the last sled load of logs. He should be here any time."

"Okay, *danki*." She turned to go back the way she had come, but Gabe stopped her. "Nancy, can I ask you something?"

"Sure."

He took a few steps closer to her. "The day Esther and I went to the clinic, you picked up a brochure on a new kind of hearing aid."

"I did. What about it?"

"Esther said she wasn't interested, but you took one, anyway. Why? Was it for Esther? Do you think it can help her?"

Nancy grew serious. "I took it for myself."

He frowned. "Are you losing your hearing? Jonah said he believed it skipped you and your sisters."

"My hearing is fine. It's just that I know that any children I have may go deaf. I want to be prepared. I want to learn as much about treatments as I can."

"I see."

She smiled. "I have told Moses about my concern. He said *Gott* decides."

"He is absolutely right and a man of strong faith. If you are discussing children, the two of you must be getting serious."

"We are. I didn't think I would like anyone that Waneta picked out for me. I was wrong. Moses is adorable."

"I never thought of him like that."

"What about you and Esther? The two of you are spending a lot of time together."

"I can't deny that I care for her, but she doesn't want me." It was painful to think the two women he had come to love in his life didn't desire him as a husband. The truth was he did love Esther, even if he couldn't admit it to anyone.

"Julia got the impression that Esther was getting very serious about you. Maybe the two of you should talk. If you need someone to sign for you to make sure she understands what you're saying, any one of us would be glad to help."

She walked off with a happy bounce in

her step. She and Moses would be well suited.

Gabe raided the kitchen for a couple of cookies and then walked into the living room. Through the window he saw Esther in the garden with her sketchbook in hand. His heart filled with love at the mere sight of her. There were things he couldn't imagine. Not having her in his life was the hardest.

Maybe he was the wrong man for her, but that must be her decision. She deserved to know that he loved her, but first he needed to apologize and rebuild her trust.

Gabe went out the door into the garden. Esther didn't notice him until his shadow fell across her. She squinted at him silhouetted against the sun. "You're back."

He moved to stand in front of her and held out his hand. "Cookie?"

She gave him a funny look but took it. *"Danki."*

He squatted on his heels and pointed

to her sketch pad. "What are you working on?"

"A few more rose sketches and some of the iris." She turned the paper so he could see.

He tapped the last rose she had drawn. "I like this one."

"So do I. What about putting it on a few of your tool belts? Women like Lilly also own tools."

He gazed into her troubled eyes. "Some men appreciate the beauty of flowers, too." He held his fist against his chest and made two circles. "I'm sorry."

"For what?"

"Acting like a cranky toddler."

A grin twitched at the corner of her mouth. "Which time?"

He smiled and nodded. "I deserved that."

"What did I do?"

That shocked him. "You didn't do anything. Yesterday I watched you signing with such eagerness. You and those other people were so fluid in your movements.

I felt awkward and left out. That must be how you feel sometimes."

"That's true."

"I've gotten used to having you all to myself. I don't begrudge you making friends. You should have more. I wanted to join the conversation, but I didn't know how. I've never felt so inadequate."

"Signing easily takes time. You are learning, Gabe."

"Not fast enough to suit me. I guess I'm impatient. Anyway, that's what caused my sour mood. And don't say 'which time.'"

"Thank you for telling me."

"I hope we can always share what's on our minds. Both *goot* and not so *goot*."

Her forgiving smile warmed his heart, but she looked away, leading him to suspect she had something else she wanted to say. He didn't have to wonder long.

"Gabe, how well do you know Danny Coblentz?"

"Pretty well, I think."

"He has upset Julia. She's leaving Saturday because of it."

"Upset her how?"

"He accused her of smearing his cousin's good name back home."

That didn't sound like his friend. "Are you sure?"

"Danny's cousin proposed to Julia last fall. She refused him. He wouldn't take no for an answer. He was constantly nagging her to change her mind. He even had his parents try to persuade her. She finally had the bishop confront him and his family. There were a lot of hard feelings. He wrote to Danny that we were coming here."

"What would you like me to do?"

"Just speak to him. Tell him Julia isn't the callous woman he believes her to be."

"I'll talk to him. Hear his side."

"That's fair enough. I don't want Julia to leave under these circumstances. I don't want her to leave at all."

"So. Are we okay now?"

"I believe we are."

"Until the next time I behave foolishly."

She tipped her head slightly. "Will there be a next time?"

"I'm pretty sure there will be. It's a hard habit to break. I wanted to ask you about a gift for Frank."

"I've thought about that, too. Any ideas?"

"How difficult would it be to make him a cowboy vest? He's getting a pony."

"Not hard at all if I have the right kind of leather."

"I may have some thin scraps you can use. We can look later."

"We may as well go look now." She held out her hand.

He rose and helped her to her feet. He didn't release her hand. Instead he twined her fingers with his. The look of longing in her eyes almost broke his control, but he didn't kiss her. Instead he began walking with her at his side. Which was exactly where he wanted her for the rest of his life.

He glanced at her face. She was looking down, but a gentle smile curved her lips.

He resisted the urge to kiss her and looked straight ahead. Their fragile relationship wasn't meant to be rushed. He squeezed her fingers. It was meant to be cherished.

Esther allowed Gabe to hold her hand as they crossed the farmyard. He wasn't a perfect man, but he was a good one. It had taken some courage to tell her he felt inadequate compared to the new Deaf friends she had made. Not every fellow could do that.

She sensed more than saw his restraint when he had helped her to her feet. She almost wished that he had kissed her. She wanted to see if it would be as breathtaking as it had been the first time. He held open the door of the workshop, and she slipped past him. If she were bold enough, she might entice him to repeat the gesture. Only she wasn't sure she had that much spice in her makeup.

The next morning Gabe brought around the buggy. His mother came out as Esther was getting in to press a box into her hands. "Just a few cinnamon rolls for them to enjoy. They are Gabe's favorite treat."

"Which explains why you are making me give them away. That's cruel, *Mamm*," he said.

"There are more for you to have later."

Gabe pointed his finger at her. "Keep Moses away from them or all I'll get are crumbs."

It was nearly fifteen miles to Heather and Randy's hobby farm. Topper's gait was unflagging as his trot ate up the miles, but it still took over an hour and a half to reach their destination.

As they pulled up in front of the house, the children came rushing out to see the horse first, and then Sophie went to Esther's door. She opened it and the child climbed up the step. Today she was wearing a yellow headband with white polka dots. "You'll never guess what Frank got for his birthday present. Never in a million years. Go ahead, guess," she said as she signed for Esther's benefit.

Esther looked at Gabe. He cupped his fingers over his chin and winked at her. "I am going to guess that he got a pony."

Sophie's eyes widened, then she smacked her forehead with her hand. "How did you know?"

"I'm sure a little birdie told him," Esther said.

Sophie's eyes narrowed. "I think it was my dad."

Randy came to take the box of cinnamon rolls from Esther and help her out of the buggy. He sniffed the packet. "This smells good."

"A gift from Gabe's mother," Esther told him.

"I believe she's someone I want to know better. Please come inside."

With Gabe beside her, Esther followed Randy into the house. The kitchen table held a cake with blue and white frosting with five candles off to the side. It had already been cut. There were smears of blue frosting on the table and glasses.

Balloons had been tied to the backs of

each chair. Polly and Frances Minor were seated at the table. Polly held a toddler on her lap. There were five other children playing a game in the living room.

Heather, looking slightly frazzled, came to greet Esther. "I'm so glad you could come," she said as she signed. Esther knew she spoke aloud for Gabe's sake, and she was grateful.

"She brought these," Randy signed and handed the box to his wife.

She lifted the lid, looked inside and set the box down. "Oh, good. More sugar. Just what the little monsters need."

The toddler on Polly's lap signed that she wanted one. Heather relented and cut her a small piece. The child's eyes lit up with delight at her first bite. She signed her thanks.

Gabe stepped close to Esther. She almost laughed at the hangdog expression on his face. "Talk about feeling inadequate. That baby signs better than I do."

She patted his arm reassuringly. "Babies can learn to sign before they learn to speak."

"Really?"

"It's true."

"I'm going to go see the new horse. At least I am something of an expert in the barn."

Esther enjoyed visiting with Polly and Frances again. She learned a lot about their programs at the school where they taught. She shared some of her concerns about the special-needs school where she worked. After discussing it, they assured her the Amish community was supplying their students with the latest curriculum and teaching tools. One by one the parents of the other children came to take them home until only Heather's children remained. Frank went outside to find his father.

Heather sat down. "I wish we had a School for the Deaf closer to us. The local school board assures us their public school can accommodate our needs, but I have some doubts. Especially for Carmen. She is easily frightened. We don't want her to regress because we've pushed her too hard. We bought this place because we wanted our children to grow up in the country and because Randy is from this area. I think we're going to homeschool the children this year or until we can find a private tutor."

Sophie and Carmen rushed to Esther's side. "We are having a tea party. Won't you join us?"

Esther saw Carmen wore a headband identical to Sophie's. Esther glanced at Heather and signed, "Is Carmen wearing her hearing aid in her headband?"

"She is, but it's turned off. She wanted to match her sister today."

Esther turned to the girls. "I would love to join your tea party." She signed as she spoke so both could understand.

Carmen took Esther's hand and tugged on it. Laughing, Esther allowed the child to lead her to their room, where they had a teapot and cups arranged on a small table with chairs. Carmen promptly took her headband off and laid it aside, messing up her fine blond hair in the process.

Sophie gave everyone a cup and began to pour the imaginary tea. Carmen passed around a plate of plastic cookies that Esther pretended to eat. The scene reminded her of how she and her sisters used to play on the kitchen floor while their mother looked on and cooked. There was always the smell of fresh-baked bread in the house.

Sophie picked up Carmen's headband. "This is for you, Esther. Carmen doesn't want it."

"Thank you, Sophie." Esther held out her hand for the gift.

"I'll put it on. I know how it goes." She slipped the headband over Esther's *kapp* and adjusted it. Esther didn't hear anything.

"Oh, I need to turn it on." Sophie touched the hearing aid. A loud squeal filled Esther's head. She flinched at the painful shock of the sound. "Turn it off."

Before Sophie touched it again, the

squealing stopped and a jumble of sounds rushed in to fill the void. Esther held her breath. She concentrated to try to identify them. Carmen was clacking two cups together. The wind whistled softly beneath the partially opened window. She heard birds outside. The sound was piercing. She hadn't heard a bird's song in years. Then she heard laughter coming from the kitchen.

Sophie looked over Esther's shoulder. "Would you like a cup of tea, sir?" Was that right? Had she heard correctly. It was so disorienting.

A deep, rumbling laugh sent chills down Esther's spine. "No, thank you. I would take a cup of coffee if you have one to go with my cinnamon roll?"

The sounds faded in and out. Esther struggled to stay upright as she grew faint.

"Sure. Here you are." Sophie carried a cup behind Esther.

"*Danki*, lovely lady."

Esther's vision blurred. She knew whose voice it was. One she had heard in her dreams but never expected to hear in her lifetime. She slowly turned around. Gabe stood sipping from his tiny cup and smiling at his hostess.

He handed the cup back to Sophie. "I've come to take my Esther home with me. Is she ready?"

Carmen patted Esther's arm. "You're crying. I don't like that thing, either."

Esther pulled off the headband and rubbed her face with both hands. "I'm ready to go. Thank you for the tea."

She kept her face down so Gabe wouldn't notice her tearstained face. In the kitchen Heather spied her and quickly came to her side. "What's wrong?"

"Nothing. I'll be fine. Thank you for the invitation. I hope Frank likes his vest. Goodbye."

She wanted to run out the door, but she walked slowly to the buggy and got in. She closed her eyes and turned her face to the window. "I'm sorry. I have a headache."

Gabe touched her arm. She couldn't

look at him. He set Topper in motion and headed home.

As the fields of potato blossoms rolled past, Esther came to grips with what had happened. She had heard Gabe's voice. The voice of the man she was falling in love with. Fresh tears threatened, but she blinked them back.

She had once met a deaf man who sometimes wore his cochlear hearing aid and sometimes didn't. When she asked him why he didn't choose one or the other, he said it didn't matter. He was a Deaf person who could sometimes hear sounds, but he was still a Deaf man.

It was the same with her. She didn't need to hear to be happy. Today had been a traumatic, painful and thankfully brief visit into the hearing world, but it had given her a gift she would cherish forever. The sound of Gabe's voice. But she was part of the Deaf community, and she wouldn't change that. They were people with a vibrant language, their own heroes, history and folk stories. God allowed her to be deaf, but He had given her much more than He had taken away.

By the time Gabe stopped the buggy, she had her emotions well in check. She turned to face him and smiled. "I'm sorry I was poor company."

"Are you better?"

"I am."

He took her hand. "I'm glad. I was worried about you."

"You needn't be."

"Maybe not, but I'd like to be the one who has the right to be concerned for you. What happened in the girls' bedroom? I saw your tears. Was it because of the hearing aid the children let you wear?"

He saw way too much. She had once told him he was observant. Now she had more proof. "I can't talk about it yet, Gabe."

"But someday?"

"Someday. I promise. Gabe, can you accept me as I am?"

"Of course. I adore you the way you are." He leaned in and kissed her forehead. "I'm the flawed one. Can you accept me?"

"Without question."

He cupped her cheek with his hand. "You're a brave woman. We have a lot more to discuss, but not right now."

She looked outside and saw they were at the school. "What are we doing here?"

"I told you I would talk to Danny. He lives beside the school. I won't be long."

"Okay. I'll be fine."

He got out and crossed to a small house on the south side of the school building. He opened the door and went inside.

He had said he would speak to Danny. She was glad he was keeping his word.

His words. *I've come to take my Esther home with me.* She recalled the exact timbre of his voice. *My Esther.*

She was—or she wanted to be—his Esther. It didn't matter that he could hear any more than it mattered that she couldn't. His heart spoke to hers.

There were going to be challenges for them, she knew that. He could be impatient. She was stubborn. They might clash on any number of subjects, but he accepted her.

She pressed both hands over her chest as joy flooded her heart. He accepted her.

# Chapter Fifteen

Gabe stepped into Danny's kitchen. His friend was washing the dishes. Danny dried his hands on a towel. "I'm ashamed to say I let them pile up until I run out of clean plates. Shall I guess why you're here?"

"Sounds like you already have an idea."

"I was rude to one of your guests. I'm not proud of the fact. I intend to apologize and beg forgiveness."

"You may not get that opportunity. I told Esther that I would speak to you and hear your side, but Julia currently plans to leave tomorrow."

Danny hung his head. "I'm sorry to hear that."

"I have come to know Julia as a sweet, modest woman. I understand you have cause to think otherwise."

"I may have been misinformed. I was shocked when I received my cousin's letters detailing his humiliation and asking me to plead his case to Julia while she was here. If she wouldn't reconsider his offer, he wanted me to make sure folks here knew she wasn't to be trusted. I believed every word he wrote, but I wasn't going to ruin her reputation. After talking to Julia, I belatedly came to realize that my cousin may have misled me. This morning I put a call through to the bishop of his district. He corroborated Julia's story. In all honesty, I never thought my cousin was capable of such behavior. I must forgive him. So must Julia. I'll come to your home this evening and beg her forgiveness."

"I don't think she'll see you."

"In that case, please assure her that I

won't bother her again. Tell her I'm sorry and I hope she can forgive me."

"I will give her your message. The family plans to stay until after the Potato Blossom Festival. Hopefully Julia will stay, too." He turned on his heels and left his friend's house, disappointed in his behavior toward Esther's sister.

Esther was waiting impatiently in the buggy. "What did he say?"

"He sends his apologies and promises not to see her again. And he asks her forgiveness. Will that be enough to keep Julia here?"

"I don't know. She was very upset. I don't want her to leave. We are finally becoming friends again."

Because it meant so much to Esther, Gabe would do his best to convince Julia to stay. "I'll speak to her."

"Thank you," she signed. "I think I'll take over Jonah's teaching duties."

He tweaked her nose. "I'd like that. A lot."

Her laughter was music to his ears. He

drove home in a happy mood. Things were looking up between them.

At the house, he stopped Topper by the front gate and turned to Esther. "Why don't you ask Julia to come see me in my workshop?"

"All right. I'll be down later to start working on the rose patterns."

"While I was in the barn with Randy today, he suggested we make some laptop carrying cases. I think the idea has merit. I'll have to find a pattern that's simple but sturdy."

"Perhaps Lilly has a laptop we can use to get dimensions."

"*Goot* idea. We can go see her tomorrow."

Gabe gave Topper a rubdown, watered him and stabled him with fresh hay. When he opened his workshop door, he found Julia waiting for him. She was sitting in Esther's chair in front of the leather stitcher.

"You wanted to speak to me?"

He leaned against his cutting table. "I went to see Danny today."

Julia pressed her lips into a tight line and tipped her head back. "I can't believe Esther involved you in this."

"She cares about you. So do I. She doesn't want you to leave. She feels she has grown closer to you and your sisters since your arrival here."

"We have. I love Esther, but I'm not going to endure the same treatment I suffered at home."

"Danny has realized he made a mistake taking his cousin's word about your behavior."

"Well, good. Better late than never," she snapped.

"He called your bishop and heard the whole story. He's ashamed and embarrassed. He has promised not to see you again. He begs your forgiveness."

"You think he means it? He won't bother me again?"

"I believe he is sincere. I've known Danny for two years. He's never done anything like this. He knows he made a mistake, and he regrets it. I hope this eases your mind enough to feel you can stay with us awhile longer."

"Ogden can be very persuasive. I should know. All right, I'll stay."

"Esther will be delighted."

She tipped her head slightly. "That's important to you, isn't it?"

"More than you know. I've made several missteps in my relationship with Esther. I don't want that to happen again. She is very dear to me."

"As long as you accept Esther for who she is without reservations, you'll do fine. If I can help in any way, please let me know."

"I may hold you to that."

The outside door opened, and Esther came in. "Are you staying, sister?"

Julia nodded. "Your young man has convinced me to remain."

"I'm so glad." She hugged her sister and then reached for his hand. She squeezed his fingers. *"Danki."*

The happiness in her eyes was all the reward Gabe could have asked for.

Over the next two days, Esther wasn't sure she had ever been so happy. She and Gabe worked side by side in the shop all day Saturday. In the evening they walked to Lilly's farm through the woods. Lilly used her computer to show Gabe what kind of carrying cases were on the market for laptops.

The off Sunday, the one without a church service, was spent in quiet reflection and Bible reading during the morning. The afternoon was devoted to visiting friends. Three local families stopped in to enjoy Talitha's cinnamon rolls and coffee. Esther's sisters and Jonah took turns signing so she was able to enjoy the company, too.

On Monday Gabe and Esther were back at work in the shop. Gabe took inventory of the leather they had available and discovered he didn't have enough to make more than one laptop case. "I reckon I'll have to take another trip into Fort Craig. I hope Ed has enough of the weight I need."

"We are low on the dyed leather for purses, too."

"I think it's best we don't go to the farmers market this Wednesday. That way will have more merchandise to take with us to the festival next week."

"Have we made enough pieces?"

"To fill our booth, yes. Will we earn enough money to make the venture worthwhile? I'm not sure."

She wanted to ease his concern. "What more can we do?"

"Keep working. I'll go to Fort Craig tomorrow. That will give us a few days yet to produce more."

"I wish we knew what would sell the best. We could concentrate on making more of those."

"Unfortunately, this first year will be mostly trial and error."

That evening Esther began teaching Gabe the sign language alphabet. Talitha joined them for her first lesson. To Esther's surprise, Waneta asked to sit in, too. Nancy and Pamela decided to instruct Moses and Seth in signing. Both couples managed to find quiet corners in the garden to practice. Esther wasn't sure how much teaching was actually accomplished.

On Tuesday morning Gabe left early for the trip into Fort Craig. Esther was stitching the last two belts when her stepmother came in. Waneta made a circuit of the room examining the machinery and boxes of items Esther had finished embellishing. She finally stopped in front of Esther's machine.

"How can you abide working in this smelly place?"

"I like the scent of leather."

"That's fortunate."

"Did you want something?"

Waneta clasped her hands together. "I believe I owe you an apology."

"For?"

"My impatience with you. Julia pointed out that I have—" She turned to the side, and Esther wasn't able to read what she was saying.

"I'm afraid you must face me, Waneta. I can't see what you're saying otherwise."

Waneta flushed bright red and stammered, "Of—of course. I was saying that I may have treated you poorly. For that I'm sorry. You may not believe it, but I love your father. He has struggled with your decision not to use your cochlear implant, and I felt I had to support him."

"I'm aware of my father's feelings."

"That being said, Talitha and I have noticed how much Gabe depends on you and how happy he seems lately. I have always liked the boy, and it's gratifying to know my decision to bring you along has met with his approval. That's really all I wanted to say. We should—" She turned away and walked out, leaving Esther wondering what it was they should do.

She shrugged and went back to sewing.

When Gabe returned in the early afternoon, bright joy filled Esther at the sight of him. She cared for him so much. She couldn't deny her feelings any longer. She loved him. He cared for her, too. She knew by the way his eyes lit up when he caught sight of her.

"Ed Carson's place was closed," he said and hung his hat on the peg by the door. He held a small package in one hand.

"You had a wasted trip. That's too bad. Will you go again tomorrow?"

"There isn't any point. He's closed until after the festival. The shopkeeper next door said he's gone to visit his daughter in New York. She just had a baby."

Gabe walked across the shop floor and sat down at his desk. He laid the package on top of it then he slumped forward with his elbows on his knees. "There isn't another tanner in the region."

"We can't get more leather?"

"I'm afraid not. This is a setback I didn't foresee."

"There's no way you could have."

"Okay. Well, my trip wasn't a complete waste of time." He picked up the package and held it out to her.

She took it gingerly. "What's this?"

"A small gift for you."

She opened it and pulled out a book. Colorful flowers adorned the cover. *"Wildflowers of Maine, Quebec and New Brunswick."* She smiled as her heart grew light at the thought of his kindness. "For me?"

"The shop next to Ed's place is a bookstore. Do you like it?"

"I love it. Now I can discover the names of the flowers I see."

"Weeds. There's an index. Look under *W.*"

She hugged it to her chest. "*Danki*. It was very thoughtful of you."

"You've worked hard without pay this past two weeks. It's only a small token of my appreciation."

"I'll treasure it always."

She was smiling now, and that was all Gabe wanted. To make her happy. "You've done enough work in here today. Let's go find out how good your book is. Maybe you can find a flower that isn't in it."

"All right. Where to?"

"The woods and then the bog. Unless you have somewhere else you'd like to explore."

"That sounds lovely. I'll get my sketch pad."

"I'll raid the kitchen for some snacks. I missed lunch."

Fifteen minutes later, they entered the cool woods behind the barn. Instead of taking the path to the Arnett farm, Gabe chose one that led toward a small clearing where an old cabin stood. He and his brothers had discovered it when they first came to Maine. It had been deserted for years, but he remembered the place being surround by flowers when he first saw it.

The path led upward into the wooded hills above New Covenant. There were several places with fine views of the mountains and the winding river below. He took Esther's hand to help her over fallen logs or boulders that jutted out of the ground. When the path widened out and they could walk side by side, he took her hand again and held it. She smiled shyly but didn't pull away.

They stopped at an opening in the trees. The valley lay spread out below in a checkered patchwork of fields and farms. She grinned. "This is beautiful."

He gazed at her face. "Yes, you are," he said softly, knowing that she wasn't looking at him.

She opened her book. "Let me see what these little white flowers are."

He took the book from her. "The better flower show is a little farther down the trail."

"If you say so, but I would like to know the name of this one."

"It's a weed."

"You have no appreciation for the simple things."

"Not when spectacular looms just around the corner."

"Lead on to this amazing scene, if you must."

He took her hand and led the way. A group of cedar trees had overgrown part of the path. He stopped there. "Cover your eyes."

"What?"

"Cover your eyes. I won't let you stumble."

She did. "What are you up to?"

He didn't answer. She couldn't see his mouth, anyway. He led her around the trees and stopped. Then he gently pulled her hands away from her face. "Not weeds."

He stepped aside. The clearing was filled with a carpet of pink, lavender, purple and white spires of lupine. She gasped and stepped out into the masses. "They're beautiful."

He moved close to her and caught her by the shoulders. "You're beautiful. I think I love you, Esther. I'm going to kiss you."

"It's about time." She smiled and circled his neck with her arms.

He pulled her close. She fit so perfectly next to him. She lifted her face to his. He couldn't resist a moment longer. He gently kissed her lips. When she didn't pull away, he cupped her head in his hands and deepened the kiss as tenderness flooded his soul. She hadn't said that she loved him, but he knew in his heart that she did. He could wait until she was ready to say the words.

Joy filled every fiber of Esther's being. She tightened her arms around Gabe's neck, drawing closer to him. His lips left hers. Before she could protest, his mouth moved across her cheek to her temple. Then he kissed her eyes and nuzzled her ear. She sighed with contentment. When he drew away, she opened her eyes. "That was better than the first time."

He chuckled. She could feel the vibrations in his chest beneath her hands. He slipped a finger under her chin and lifted her face. "Practice makes perfect."

"Then we should practice some more." She planted a peck on his lips.

He held her away. "It's a long walk back, and we still have work to do."

"Did I mention that my arm and shoulder ache from working the lever on the stitcher so much?"

"I can take over now that my arm is better. Any other excuses? A headache, perhaps?"

"My head is fine. Thank you for bringing me here. This is lovely."

"I knew you'd like it."

Together they started back to the house. Halfway there she saw Pamela and Seth strolling toward them.

Esther smiled at her sister. "The view is lovely up ahead, but go all the way to the little cabin."

"I know." Pamela slanted a glance at Seth. "We've been there already."

"Is Gabe a good kisser?" Pamela signed. "Your lips are a little puffy."

Esther touched them with one finger. The feel of Gabe's kiss lingered there still. She cast a covert glance his way. "He's good, but he needs more practice."

Pamela burst out laughing while Gabe and Seth looked on with confused expressions. She linked her arm with Seth and drew him along the path.

Gabe arched one eyebrow as he stared at Esther. "What did you say?"

"It was just a little sisterly gossip."

He took her hand and walked on. When they came around the barn, Esther saw a car parked in front of the house. She recognized it as the one Mr. Jefferson had driven away in. He appeared to be in a heated discussion with Zeke as Asher and Moses stood behind their father.

She looked up at Gabe. "What's going on?"

"I don't know."

As they drew closer, Mr. Jefferson caught sight of her. He pointed. "She's the one. She took my order. I needed those harnesses today."

Zeke turned to Esther. "Did you take an order from this man for six parade harnesses?"

"No. He came into the workshop. I told

him Gabe was out cutting wood. I asked if he wanted to leave a message. I searched for a pen and paper. When I found them and looked up, he was leaving."

"So you didn't hear me say I needed eight parade harnesses like the one you folks showed me by today? If you people can't get the work done, then I'll take my business elsewhere."

Esther's heart was about to pound out of her chest. "I didn't hear you because I'm Deaf, sir. I can lip-read, but only if you are looking at me."

His anger deflated. "Oh. Well, how was I to know? Why didn't you say something?"

"You didn't give me the chance."

"I'm sorry about that, but you shouldn't be working where folks expect verbal orders to be taken. I could sue you people for breach of contract."

Zeke scowled. "A handshake is how we seal a contract, Mr. Jefferson. That's the way we do business. If there was no handshake, there was no deal."

"You Amish." Hank Jefferson stomped off to his car and drove away.

Esther pressed a hand to her cheek as she looked at Gabe. "I've cost you thousands of dollars in lost business. I'm so sorry."

Zeke laid a hand on her shoulder. "*Gott* allowed it. Who are we to question His will?" He walked into the barn. Asher and Moses followed him.

Gabe seemed to sag under the weight of what had happened. "It would have made all the difference, but—"

She didn't catch what else he said, for he had started walking away. She followed him to the workshop. He went to the desk and sat down with his head in his hands.

"I'm sorry."

He shrugged and looked up. "It was my fault as much as yours. I have invoice order forms. I should have told you about them and put them out for you to use."

He pulled open the desk drawer. His hand froze in midair. He slowly lifted out a piece of paper and looked at her. "This is something else I've been meaning to speak to you about."

She saw it was a brochure like the ones in the doctor's office about hearing aids. Esther took a step back. Pain shot through her chest. She couldn't breathe. *Not again. Don't let it happen again, God.* "No! No. Put it away. Better yet, throw it in the trash."

His eyes were full of confusion and disappointment. "Tell me why you won't at least consider this option? It's not the same as a cochlear implant. Don't you want to hear?"

"I am as *Gott* made me. I'm Deaf. I'm not broken. I don't need to be fixed. Do you understand me? I'm not broken! I thought you loved me." Tears began streaming down her cheeks.

He took a step toward her with his hand out. "Esther, I do love you, but I don't understand."

She moved back out of his reach. "Then it's not the kind of love I want."

She spun around and ran out of the building.

# Chapter Sixteen

Gabe paced at the foot of the stairs until Julia appeared at the top of them. It was Esther he wanted to see. Needed to see. She had retreated to her bedroom yesterday, and she hadn't come down since. It was almost noon.

"How is she?" he asked.

"Surprisingly calm." Julia came down the stairs.

"Will she see me?"

Julia sadly shook her head. "She won't."

"I have to see her. I have to make her understand. I was disappointed by what happened, but I don't blame her."

"She blames herself for the loss of Mr. Jefferson's business. She knows how important it was to you."

"I don't care about his business. I care about Esther." He turned around and paced across the hall and back. "She has to talk to me eventually."

"*Nee*, she doesn't. She sent Jonah to Lilly Arnett."

"For what reason?"

"She needs a ride to the bus station in Fort Craig this afternoon. She's leaving."

Gabe sank onto the bottom step and cupped his hands over the back of his neck. "She can't do that."

Julia patted his shoulder. "You don't know my sister as well as you think you do. She can and she will travel by bus all the way home to Millersburg, Ohio, by herself unless I go with her."

He looked up at Julia. "Tell me what I can do to change her mind," he pleaded.

"I honestly don't know. She has been deeply hurt, but it is frightening how calm she is."

"I don't believe this is happening. How could it have all gone so wrong?"

"That's something only you can answer."

He looked up the stairwell. He wanted to shout Esther's name, make her see him, but no matter how loudly he called for her, she would never hear it. And that was part of his fear. She could shut him out completely whenever she wanted.

He heard a car drive up outside. If it was Lilly, maybe he could talk her out of taking Esther to the bus station. He went to the window and saw it was Heather and Randy. Asher came in. "There's a couple here who want to purchase a harness for their pony. Do you know anything about it?"

"They are friends of Esther's. Would you be interested in training a pony to pull a cart?"

"Sure. Little horses don't hurt as much when they step on your foot."

His brother was trying to be funny, but Gabe didn't see the humor in anything.

"I'll speak to them." He wasn't doing himself or the family any good keeping vigil at the foot of the stairs.

Heather smiled brightly at him. "We have decided there will be less squabbling over the pony if the children can all ride in a cart together."

"It's a *goot* plan."

"Do you need to take measurements for the harness?" Randy asked.

"*Nee*, I've seen your fellow. My pony-size harness will fit him fine. There is plenty of room to make adjustments in the straps."

Heather glanced toward the house. "Where is Esther?"

"Avoiding me."

"Oh. That doesn't sound good."

"She's leaving Maine today."

Zeke walked up. "What is this?"

Gabe nodded. "Esther is leaving."

"I'm sorry, *sohn*." Zeke laid a hand on Gabe's shoulder. Gabe had to fight back tears.

"I'm sorry, too," Heather said. "What happened, if it is any of my business?"

Maybe Heather could shine some light on Esther's behavior. She was familiar with a few Deaf people. He repeated what had happened as best he could. "I still don't understand why she refused to consider a hearing aid. Surely it would make life so much easier for her."

Heather sighed heavily. "I've done a lot of reading about the Amish since I met you and Esther. I just don't get you people."

Gabe and Zeke frowned.

"What harm is there in using electricity? You shortchange your children by denying them advanced education. Why not allow them to go to high school and college? You are setting them up to fail in our society.

"You cling to things that have no purpose. Your language is a case in point. Why use a means of communication that only other Amish can understand? You live in America with millions of Americans. Yes, you learn English in school, but that isn't the language you prefer to speak. *Deitsh* is how you define yourself. It's what you teach your children when they are growing up. You revere the stories of the men and women who were martyred for your faith, but is that important in this day and age? I don't see that it is. You could easily become part of this world."

"An outsider cannot understand our ways," Zeke said.

"But things would be so much easier for you if you gave up your antique way of life. Have I made my point, Gabe?"

His mind was churning. "It isn't easy for me to accept that Esther can turn her back on something that would allow her to hear. That she would prefer to remain deaf."

"I may not understand the Amish, but I respect you. The way you live is your choice. It doesn't make sense to me. I couldn't go a single day without using my cell phone or computer. You have the right to live as you choose without anyone making you feel guilty or inferior. You are different, but I don't truly see that you need to be fixed. The Deaf culture has their own language—they have their own heroes and history, their own way of caring for others like themselves. Many of them accept God's will in everything. Sound familiar?"

"A little," he admitted. "How do I convince Esther that I finally understand when she won't even look at me?"

"You are going to need some help," Julia said as she came up behind him.

Esther decided to wait for Lilly in the garden. She had grown tired of crying into her pillow. Flowers had always been her comfort. She needed comfort today. She struggled to hold back her tears as she sat on a wooden bench. She loved Gabe, but he didn't see her as a whole person. There was no way to describe the pain and humiliation she felt. All she could hope was that distance would bring some relief.

She stood and wrapped her arms tightly

across her middle as if she could hold back her disappointment. She paced across the garden. Why wasn't Lilly here yet? How much longer would she have to wait?

Esther turned back toward the house and saw him standing beside his mother's rose-covered trellis. "Please go away." She couldn't bear this. Not now. Not when she was so close to making her escape.

He held up one hand. "Please hear what I have to say."

She closed her eyes. She couldn't give him another chance to hurt her. She thought he would go away, but instead she found herself enveloped in his arms. She pressed her hands against his chest, but she couldn't bring herself to push him away. In spite of everything, she still loved him. She still needed him.

His lips moved softly against her temple. He was saying something. She turned her face away. "You need to let me go. The car will be here soon."

When he didn't release her, she opened

her eyes. Tears glistened on his eyelashes and left a trail down his cheeks. "Don't go."

She could hear the echo of his voice in her mind. He stepped away from her. "Don't go," he signed.

"I'm not broken. I am the way God made me. Why couldn't you accept that?"

"You aren't broken. I am. I'm incomplete without you at my side, Esther. You are the better part of me. If you go, you will leave a wreck of a man behind. I'm sorry I hurt you. Heather was here, and she helped me to understand. I didn't know."

Esther turned away from the pain in his eyes. She wanted to believe him. She wasn't sure she could. "It's too late, Gabe."

He took her gently by the shoulders and turned her around. "Is it too late for forgiveness?"

"Of course not. I forgive you." She meant it. In her heart she knew he hadn't intended to hurt her. He had only been trying to help, but it was help she didn't need and didn't want.

"Forgiveness is a first—first step—"
He shook his head. "I—I can't do this."
He looked over Esther's shoulder. "Julia,
please help me."

Esther saw her sister walk up beside
him. A wry smile curved Julia's mouth.
"He's a little overcome with emotion. He's
afraid you won't hear everything he needs
to say," she signed.

Esther raised her chin and looked at
him. "I'm listening."

"Okay. I knew from the day we met that
you were the most amazing woman. I fell
in love with you the morning you went
back to the pond to see the moose. I tried
to deny it, but the harder I fought the more
embedded you became in my heart."

He looked down. Esther watched Julia
to see what he was saying.

"I was scared, Esther. I tried to imagine a life with you. I knew I could learn
to sign, but how long would it take me
to be able to speak as freely as Heather
and her friends? A year? Two? How many
times would you miss what I was saying

because I spoke too fast or wasn't looking at you?"

He raised his face to her. "How can I whisper that I love you in the dark when I'm holding you in my arms? How can I warn you of danger? All these things went through my head. In spite of my fears, I still wanted you in my life. When I learned about the bone-anchored hearing aid, I thought it was the answer for me. For the things I feared. I never asked if it was the answer for you. And for that I'm truly sorry."

Julia wiped a tear from her eye. "He deserves another chance, sister," she signed.

"I'm thinking about it," Esther signed back.

Julia smiled sadly. "One of us should be happy."

"Am I missing something?" Gabe asked.

Esther didn't need her sister to tell her what he said. "Thank you, Julia. You are a wonderful sister, but I can take it from here."

Julia gripped Esther's hand, then patted Gabe's shoulder and walked into the house.

Esther took both Gabe's hands in hers. "I did not consider your fears any more than you thought about mine. We really are going to have to work on our communication skills."

"I'm willing to do anything you ask."

She put her hand in his and began to spell. "This is how you say 'I love you' in the dark. Or this way." She pressed her lips softly at the corner of his mouth and whispered the words she wanted so badly to say. "I love you, Gabriel Fisher."

He took a step back and began to sign, "Flower, will you marry me?"

Esther drew a sharp breath, unable to speak for the tightness in her throat.

Disappointment filled his eyes. "Is that a no?"

She swallowed hard. "You used my sign name. That's the first time."

"But not the last. Will you marry me, Flower? I love you," he signed.

"Our children may be deaf."

"They will have an amazing mother to inspire and teach them."

"I won't hear you shout if I'm in danger."

"I'll keep throwing myself in front of trucks to protect you."

She folded her arms. "We will disagree."

"We'll make up."

"My deafness cost you thousands of dollars in lost work."

"I'll take it out of your wages. You'll have to sew for me for the next sixty or seventy years."

"Gabe, I'm serious. I know how badly you want to keep your family together."

"My brothers and I are grown men. We will do what needs to be done. Even if that means leaving for a while."

"I reckon I'm all out of objections."

His eyes lit up. "Really? You'll marry me? You will love, honor and obey me until death do us part?"

"About the obey part."

He stepped close and took her hands. "Will you love, honor and cherish me?"

"I can agree to that."

"*Goot.* I will be the head of the house. You be the heart. My heart."

"I'm going to marry you, but only because I can't live without you."

"I'll take what I can get." He drew her into his arms. Where she belonged and never wanted to leave. His lips touched the corner of her mouth. She knew exactly what he was saying when he whispered, "I love you."

"*Gott* is great," she whispered back. "He has brought me my one true love. I love you, Gabe Fisher."

He drew back to look at her. "I have waited and longed to hear those words. Say them again."

She cupped his cheek. "I love you, Gabe."

He blew out a deep breath. "Finally. It was worth the wait. I pray you never grow tired of saying it."

She pulled him close. "Oh, I won't. I can promise you that," she said as she kissed his pretty mouth again.

# *Epilogue*

The first day of the Potato Blossom Festival was a whirlwind of excitement. There was a parade, a carnival, games, livestock shows and children everywhere. Esther took a moment between customers in Gabe's booth to gaze at him and wonder what their children would look like. Hopefully like him. He had the most beautiful mouth.

He waved his hand in front of her face. "Where are you?"

"Admiring the man I love."

"Talk like that and I'll start kissing you."

"I'm okay with that."

She was a little disappointed he didn't make good on his promise. Instead he pointed to a nearby booth. "I see Seth and Pamela."

Esther sighed. "They look so happy. I'm glad she said yes when he proposed."

"That's two engagements this summer. I reckon *Mamm* and Waneta's plan worked out pretty well after all."

Esther grinned at him. "In spite of our resistance to their matchmaking."

He smiled. "Thankfully we both had a change of heart. Are we out of purses?"

"We have one left in the box in back. I'll get it." Gabe had been taking care of the customers while Esther kept the display case and shelves stocked.

She stepped out to the counter with the last pink rose-embossed purse when she saw who the customer was.

"Heather. How are you?"

"In need of your help," she signed.

"What can I do?"

"I need a nanny-slash-tutor for my children. Please tell me you are available."

Esther couldn't believe what she was hearing. Her only regret about her upcoming marriage to Gabe was that she would have to give up her position in the special-needs school back home. "Let me ask Gabe."

Since Amish women rarely worked outside the home after marrying, she wanted to be sure he was okay with it. Not that she wouldn't take the job. She wasn't married yet.

Heather grinned. "I already spoke to him. He agreed it would be a fine idea. I don't know why I didn't think of it sooner. Randy and I will pick you up and take you home so you don't have to worry about driving a buggy so far. The kids love the idea."

So did Esther. "Where is Gabe?"

Heather pointed toward the side of the booth. "He stepped out to talk to a man I don't know."

Esther leaned over the counter and saw Gabe with Mr. Jefferson. The two men shook hands. Jefferson walked away, and

Gabe came into the booth with a huge grin on his face.

"What did he want?" she asked, not sure she wanted to hear anything about the man.

"It seems none of the other harness makers in the area can beat my prices. He had to eat crow, but it wasn't as painful for him as having to part with an extra thousand dollars. I've got an order for an eight-horse full parade hitch."

She clasped her hands together. "Gabe, that's wonderful. I take back all my bad thoughts about the man."

"Me, too. At least until his check clears the bank." He gave her a sheepish look. "I shouldn't have said that. I have forgiven him. Are you going to work for Heather?"

"I am. Are you sure you don't mind?"

"You are free to do as you please within the rules of our church. That obey thing with me won't kick in until November."

She grabbed his hand and squeezed. "I can hardly wait."

"You haven't seen northern Maine in

winter. We can get up to five feet of snow. You may regret your choice."

She winked at him. "Snowbound with my new husband. However will I manage?"

"Very well, I think," he said as he pulled her into the back of the booth where they wouldn't be seen and proceeded to kiss her breathless.

\* \* \* \* \*

Dear Reader,

I hope you found my story to be informative, entertaining and sweet. I enjoyed learning about the Deaf culture in my research. That's Deaf with a capital *D*. It is a culture every bit as interesting as the Amish people I normally write about.

I have tried to be accurate and sensitive to the Deaf in my telling of this story. I would like to thank Elsa Sjunneson for her help. Her insight was extremely helpful. I am not deaf. Nor do I personally know anyone who is. The emotions and conflict between Esther and Gabe have come wholly from my imagination. Errors or misinformation I have shared are entirely my own fault.

I love being back in New Covenant, Maine. It's a state that is dear to my heart and very far from my Kansas farm. If you haven't visited Maine, you should. It has a wild beauty that feeds the soul.

I hope you and yours are well. As I write

this story, I am shut in my home because of the COVID-19 virus. I've been praying for the country and the world. I look forward to the day this is over. Maybe by the time you read these words, it will be. There, that's my hope and my prayer.

Blessings,
*Patricia Davids*